BRAND OF FURY

BRAND OF FURY

JACK BARTON

CUTTING EDGE

Jack Barton was a pseudonym of writer Joseph L. Chadwick.

ISBN-13: 978-1-954840-53-9

Published by
Cutting Edge Books
PO Box 8212
Calabasas, CA 91372
www.cuttingedgebooks.com

CHAPTER ONE

They came upon him working alone in a lonely place, as skillful at his furtive trade as a cow thief needed to be, and so intent at the moment that he was unaware of being watched. The bawling of the yearling under the red hot bite of the running iron kept him from hearing their approach.

They reined in at the rim of the rock-and-brush screened hollow. Ed Raglan said, "Cover me, Tip. But if you have to shoot, make it a warning shot. I don't want him killed."

He swung from the saddle and worked his way down into the hollow, while Tip Nolan, with a hothead's scowl for this fooling around with a rustler caught in the act, drew his rifle from its boot and jacked a cartridge into the firing chamber.

The rustler, his back to Raglan, removed piggin' string and his own weight from the yearling, and the beast scrambled to its feet and went off in wild flight, still bawling mournfully.

Raglan said, "You're quite a hand with that iron, friend. Quite an artist."

The rustler gave a violent start, then whirled, a lanky scarecrow of a man badly in need of a bath and a bar-bering. He was not a stranger to Raglan, and in a moment his name came to mind: Will Vance.

Vance said, "Nothing to it, on a maverick."

"That yearling was no maverick."

"Your eyes played tricks on you, mister."

"I know my own outfit's brand, even when it's been blotched," Raglan said. "Friend, you changed that Seventy-seven into a Ladder A."

Vance was defiant. "I'm not admitting that."

"It could be proved easy enough."

"And if it is?"

Raglan kept his voice civil, only mildly rebuking. "It's become the custom in these parts to hang men caught brand blotting. Or haven't you heard?"

He saw his words take the starch of defiance out of the man, but then desperation came to Vance. He swung the running iron up for a clubbing blow and leaped across the half dozen feet of ground separating them. Tip Nolan's rifle cracked from the rim of the hollow. The slug shrieked past Vance's head and brought him to an abrupt halt. The rustler's scrawny neck swiveled as he stared around and up at the second 77 rider. Then he let the iron fall to the ground.

He sighed resignedly. "All right, Raglan—damn you!"

"Looks like you've got to be taught a lesson, friend."

"At the end of a hangrope, eh?"

Raglan considered a moment, wondering about the extent of Vance's guilt. He decided that it was less than it appeared, but a part of the guilt did lie with the man, and it wouldn't do to let him off scot free. Raglan called, "Tip, keep out of this." He motioned toward the running iron. "You wanted to use that on me, Vance. Go ahead. I'm giving you your chance. Pick it up, man."

Vance frowned with bewilderment, then a look of shyness came to his eyes. He shrugged, and said, "Whatever you say," and dived for the iron.

Raglan let him get hold of the thing, which could well turn out to be a deadly weapon, but before Vance could come erect, he put a foot against the man's shoulder and sent him sprawling in the dust. Vance bounded up catlike and made a vicious swipe at Raglan's legs. Dodging the blow, Raglan closed with him and got his own hold on the iron. They strained against each other for possession of the weapon, falling to the ground in a savage wrestling. Raglan finally wrenched it from Vance's grasp, then rose and flung it as far as he could.

Vance cursed, picked himself up, rushed. He staggered Raglan with one of his wild punches, catching the 77 man between the eyes. As Raglan reeled off balance, the rustler drove a knee at his groin. Pivoting, Raglan took it on his thigh, then halted Vance's attack with a blow to the jaw. He battered Vance at will now, methodically and without anger, until the man, bloody and dazed, dropped to hands and knees.

Raglan stood over him, waiting. "Enough of a lesson?"

He was tall, whip-lean and so durable that the exertion of roughing up the rustler caused his deep chest to heave hardly at all. He was big-boned, bronzed of skin, yellow-haired, gray of eyes, handsome in a rugged fashion. He had about him the air of a man who was master of himself and of his own world, meaning the 77 Ranch. Because he ramrodded 77, and because of that sense of mastery, he felt no satisfaction in having whipped Will Vance. It had been an unpleasant task he'd given himself—but also the lesser of what he considered two evils.

Vance heaved over onto his rump. He sat there wiping the smear of blood, sweat and dirt from his face and looking up with clearing eyes in which pain and hatred mingled. "All right," he growled. "You've had your fun and I've had my lesson."

"Friend, the Vigilantes would have made the lesson a lot more final."

Hatred faded from Vance's eyes, and comprehension replaced it. He picked up his hat, struggled to his feet and stood swaying.

"So it was either be licked or be hanged," he said. "I heard you were a fair man, Raglan. Now I know it."

"Just don't let me catch you with a running iron again."

"I can go?"

"Yeah. And you'd better keep going, right off this range," Raglan told him. "There's a witness, and he won't keep this to himself. Once the Vigilantes have your name, you'll be a marked man. If I were you, friend, I wouldn't even stop at Ladder A for the five dollars Frank Amberton owes you for changing the brand on that yearling."

Vance said, "You're a sharp one too, Raglan," and went limping to his horse.

It was a stocky roan cowpony, a fine animal, but its rigging was as disreputable as its owner's clothes. Vance, obviously down on his luck, had turned to rustling to keep body and soul together. Raglan felt a little sorry for him.

Vance coiled his rope and mounted. He said, "You won't catch me again, Raglan," wheeled the roan about, and headed south across the range at a lope.

Raglan climbed to the hollow's rim and mounted his dun horse. He took out makings and built a smoke. Lighting the cigarette, he saw Tip Nolan's disapproving scowl. Tip was young and intolerant, full of a violent hatred for rustlers.

Raglan said, "A nice shot, Tip. It saved me a broken head."

"I should have put it closer, right between his eyes."

"What would that have got you?"

"One less rustler."

"And maybe a lot of sleepless nights."

"Not me. Killing a cow thief wouldn't bother my conscience."

Raglan took a long drag on his cigarette, showing more annoyance with Tip Nolan than he had with Will Vance. "In that case, bucko, maybe you'd better change outfits. Matthew Dane likes trigger-quick hombres in his Tomahawk crew."

Tip squirmed in the saddle. "Hell, I'm not sour on Seventy-seven Ranch. It's just that you're not rough enough on rustlers. That Will Vance—"

"Forget him. He'll not work over any more brands on this range."

"You hope. What did he change that yearling's brand to?"

Raglan was slow to answer, and finally he decided on less than the truth. "I don't know that I noticed." He deadened the cigarette and dropped it. "You head back to ranch headquarters, Tip. I'm going to town and get duded up for that party at Tomahawk tonight."

Tip Nolan's tough young face took on a scowl. "That Matt Dane," he said. "What's he think he is, not inviting the cowhands from the neighboring outfits when he throws a shindig? Does he figure he's upper class or something?" He gave Raglan a resentful look. "How come you rate an invite when the rest of us Seventy-seven hands don't? You're only a hired hand, even if you are foreman."

Raglan laughed, but behind his words was a definite seriousness. "I'm wondering that, too," he said. "Why I rate an invitation." He lifted his dun's reins, added, "See you, Tip," and turned away.

He rode slowly south, still wondering—for Matthew Dane hated the sight of him.

He held the dun to a walk, and after perhaps ten minutes he reined it about and brought it to a stop. He could see Tip already far to the north, traveling at a steady lope. Satisfied that the young rider would continue on to 77 headquarters, Raglan stood in his stirrups and peered about the range. He spotted the yearling which had undergone the brand blotting at Will Vance's hands, and turned toward it.

He removed his rope from his saddle, shook out the loop, and kept his horse walking in on the critter. The yearling set out in sudden flight, but he had no trouble roping it. He kept his lariat tied hard and fast, and so dropped from the saddle the instant the yearling was caught. The dun held the rope taut, and Raglan bull-dogged the young steer to the ground. He examined Vance's handiwork, making sure that the original 77 mark had been changed into a Ladder A. It wasn't a matter in which there was room for doubt, for he'd already decided to approach Frank Amberton about the brand blotting. Now, sure of the Ladder A brand, he removed the loop and let the yearling scramble up and run. He remained hunkered down there, building a smoke and thinking about it.

He was not greatly surprised.

Suspicion of Frank Amberton of the Ladder A had come to him some time ago, but until today he'd not been sure—and had hoped he never would be. For Frank and he had known each other a long time, and if he had any friend, it was Frank Amberton. They'd known each other from their Texas days. Of course, they'd followed different trails since settling in Wyoming. Frank had founded a sizable ranch and prospered—prospered perhaps inordinately—and also he had married and settled down. But their friendship hadn't ended. It was merely neglected. And friendship, Raglan told himself, demanded that he give Frank a warning.

He wondered uneasily how he was to go about it. He couldn't just say, "Look, bucko, I know you're a thief and you'd better quit your stealing before somebody else finds you out." It wasn't that simple.

In the beginning, Frank probably had done exactly what the other outfits did. They all followed the custom of paying their riders five dollars for every maverick—or slick, as an unbranded cow critter was often called here in the Territory—put into their own outfit's brand. The 77 outfit did it. So did Tomahawk. Ladder A had the same privilege, but Frank Amberton had gone a step farther. He had made a deal with men not on his payroll, Will Vance for one, and thus gained more than his fair share of the mavericks. But evidently he hadn't been satisfied with the number of mavericks being put into his Ladder A brand, and so now he had his maverickers doing an occasional job of brand blotting when they felt there was no risk of getting caught.

But Will Vance had been caught, and, by the same token, Frank Amberton was caught.

Raglan sighed, rose, walked to his horse and coiled his rope.

He rode south again, heading into the Hatchet Hills. From this part of the range the shortest route to town was through the hills, through the country where the two-bit nester outfits operated. These little cowmen were the men being blamed by the big outfits for the rustling, and that, it seemed to Ed Raglan, made it all the worse for Frank Amberton to be a rustler. Frank's Ladder A was considered a big outfit and Frank was looked upon as a respectable rancher. In fact, Frank talked loudest against the thievery of the nesters and quite likely he was one of the night-riding Vigilante band.

Once in the hills, Raglan descended into the little valley where a nester named Chronister ran his little ranch. He headed across the valley, lifting his dun to a lope. He saw nothing of Chronister on the range, and swung close to the man's log buildings to call a howdy to him. He was on fairly friendly terms with most of the two-bit ranchers, despite his being ramrod of 77. Before taking the foreman job with the big outfit, he had been one of them with a camp on Squaw Creek. In fact, he still had cattle in his RAG iron.

He passed the log buildings without seeing Chronister, but a short distance beyond them, when about to ford the creek, he saw a paint pony standing ground-hitched near a huge old cottonwood. A moment later he saw Luke Chronister, and horror gripped him.

Chronister hung from a limb of the tree with a rope around his neck, his feet nearly touching the ground and his lifeless body in slight motion as a vagrant breeze made a grotesque pendulum of it.

Raglan reined in. He didn't want to see this at all, but he couldn't wrench his gaze away.

After a moment a sound reached his stunned mind, a sound of sobbing.

CHAPTER TWO

He saw her then, sitting on a rock at the edge of the creek a little distance beyond the hang-tree. He rode to her and dismounted. She was from one of the nester ranches, a back-country girl. She was wearing the same sort of range clothes a man wore, from hat to boots. At the moment her hat hung at her shoulders by its chin strap, and the breeze was toying with her red-brown hair.

So far as he remembered, Raglan had never seen her before, but he recalled talk among the 77 hands about a Mallory girl who was something of a beauty. He knew this must be she, for Luke Chronister had had no family.

She was close to hysteria, and for a while she seemed unaware of him. Finally her sobbing stopped, and she sat there hunched over, covering her face with her hands.

She said huskily, "Won't you please take him down from there?"

Raglan said, "Yes," and turned away.

With his pocketknife, he cut the rope and eased the body to the ground. He noticed the paper then, thrust under one of Chronister's suspenders. He knew what it meant before he reached for it, but he needed to make sure. It was a piece of brown wrapping-paper, and the message was crudely painted in red: a skull and crossbones and the numerals 3-7-77.

The sign of the Vigilantes.

He crumbled the paper, shoved it into his pocket, then went to the cabin for a blanket. After covering the body, he returned to the girl. She had herself under control now. At least, she no longer sobbed. But when she looked at Raglan there was still a sign of shock in her eyes. He could understand her being upset. Hardened as he was, it had unnerved him to find Luke Chronister like that.

"You're all right now?" he asked.

"I don't think I'll ever be all right again," she said tonelessly. "How could they do such a thing? How could they?"

He had no answer to that, but supposed the Vigilantes could, justify their action.

The girl said, "A few days ago he came by our place and asked me to patch a shirt for him. I was returning it this morning—and found him like that."

"You're a Mallory? Sam Mallory's daughter?"

"Yes. I'm Christine Mallory."

"Want me to see you home, Christine?"

"No, thank you. He—he shouldn't be left alone."

"He won't know whether he's alone or not," Raglan said. "Anyway, I'll come back and dig a grave."

She stared, as though really seeing him for the first time. Something in her manner told him that he'd unwittingly said the wrong thing. She rose abruptly. "We back country people bury our own dead," she said. "I know you. You're Ed Raglan from Seventy-seven Ranch. You're one of them."

He said, "No, I'm not one of them," but she had already swept past him and was running toward the paint pony.

He strode after her, catching hold of the paint's bridle as she mounted.

He said, "I had no part in what happened here. I work for Seventy-seven, but that doesn't mean that I ride with the

Vigilantes." He didn't know the reason for it, but somehow it was important that he make this girl, this Christine Mallory,. believe that. "If I'd had a part in it, I wouldn't have come by here today. I knew Luke Chronister. I liked him. If he was a rustler, I didn't know it."

"I'm going after my menfolks, Raglan," she said. "You'd better clear out before they come to bury Luke. That's all I have to say to you."

"I tell you—"

"Turn my horse loose!"

"All right. But only after you act reasonable."

"What am I to do? Am I to say that this horrible thing is right?"

He realized that nothing he could say would change her mind about him. Maybe she had a right to blame everybody connected with the big outfits. Besides, it hardly mattered what she thought of him. He said, "I'm sorry," and stepped back so she could ride away.

She struck out at a lope, riding as expertly as a cowhand, and Raglan watched admiringly until she disappeared through a gap in the hills. He mounted his dun and continued toward the town of Bennett, thinking it wise to heed her warning about not being there when she returned with her menfolks. They too would believe that he'd had a hand in hanging Luke Chronister, and he wanted no trouble with the Mallorys.

After leaving the valley, he reined in and built a smoke and took out the paper he'd found on Chronister's body. He frowned at the grim legend, a warning to other rustlers that they would be dealt with in the same fashion as Luke Chronister. The skull and crossbones was the ancient symbol of death. The numbers, 3-7-77, were the dimensions of a grave: three by seven feet, by seventy-seven inches.

This calling card of the Vigilantes was not something new. The men who were taking the enforcement of law and order into their own hands here on the Tulare Basin range had borrowed the warning symbols from the citizens' committees of the Montana mining camps during the campaign against outlawry some years earlier. They had been used in various parts of the Wyoming and Montana cattle country within the past several years, in the eternal feud between the big outfits and the small ranchers. It was, to Ed Raglan's mind, a vicious instrument.

He disapproved of the whole Vigilante idea. To him it seemed a worse evil than the crime it attempted to put down. Hanging was too severe a punishment for the few cattle that Luke Chronister may have stolen.

He returned the paper to his pocket, not sure why he was keeping it or why he had taken it off Chronister's body. He had no idea of using it to unmask the Vigilante band. He already could guess at the identity of the members. Matthew Dane was almost certainly the ringleader, and Frank Amberton probably was one of his followers, and Lyle Creighton, manager of 77 Ranch, could be another. Name the boss of any big outfit, Raglan thought, and you'd be naming a Vigilante.

Reaching Bennett, he stabled his horse at the Star Corral and went to Herb Glennon's barber shop for a shave and haircut. From the barber's, he went to the Welcome Cafe for dinner and found Bart Somers, a former Tomahawk puncher, at the counter. Somers was a coarsely handsome man in his late twenties, and, to Raglan's mind, possessed of a wild streak. He had an easy grin, a devil-may-care manner. He winked at Raglan over the rim of his coffee cup.

"What ails you, Ed? You're as sour looking as a man with money."

Raglan took the stool next to Somers. "What's there to be happy about, Bart?"

"That's easy to answer. Be dumb and you'll be happy."

"You never struck me as dumb."

Somers laughed. "Still, I'm happy."

Raglan told the counterman to bring him fried ham and eggs and coffee. He gave Bart Somers a curious look and decided that the man was happy enough, probably because he took nothing seriously. Somers had been a tophand at Tomahawk until about six months ago, when Matthew Dane had fired and blacklisted him so that he couldn't land a job with any other big outfit. Dane had caught the puncher burning his own brand instead of Tomahawk's on a maverick. Raglan had no idea of what Somers had been doing since, but suspected it was rustling. That was how a man's mind worked nowadays, Raglan reflected; he suspected everybody but himself of being a thief.

Bart Somers said, "You sure smell pretty, Ed. Slicked up for the party at Tomahawk tonight?"

"That's it."

"Wouldn't mind being at the shindig, myself."

"Maybe you shouldn't have had that fall-out with Matthew Dane."

Somers chuckled. "Maybe I shouldn't," he said. "But even if I was on Tomahawk's payroll, it wouldn't mean I'd be invited to his party. Dane won't have any of his cowhands present, you can bet." He finished his coffee. "Do something for me, Ed. Give my regards to Laurie Dane, eh?"

"Sure, Bart."

"There's a real gal, that Laurie."

"She's trouble, friend."

Somers gave him a sly look. "So you found out, didn't you?"

Raglan smiled. Three years ago, when he was ranching on his own, Laurie Dane had got a crush on him. She'd been seventeen then, too young for a man to become involved with and too young to know her own mind. When Matthew Dane found out that his daughter was interested in a man, he'd hit the ceiling. He'd come to Raglan's place on Squaw Creek with the idea of running him out of the country. Raglan hadn't scared. He'd made an enemy of Matthew Dane by standing up to him—and by telling him to keep his daughter at home. Dane had backed down, perhaps for the first time in his life. Instead of driving Raglan off the range, he'd sent Laurie to school in the East. She'd been away for more than two years, and returned a spoiled brat of a girl no longer. She didn't have any interest in Ed Raglan now, so far as he knew, but her father still hadn't forgiven him for being defiant.

Raglan said, "Don't try to make something out of nothing, friend. I didn't play along with Laurie, and so there was no real trouble for me. Matthew Dane and I are still on speaking terms— when he can't get out of speaking to me."

"And you're invited to the birthday party he's giving for Laurie."

"That makes you wonder, does it?"

Somers smiled. "It does." He flipped a coin onto the counter to pay for his meal and got down from his stool. Then, nudging Raglan with an elbow he said, "If I was going to that shindig, I wouldn't be going around with that sour look, bucko. Or haven't you seen Laurie since she came back from the East?"

"I've seen her," Raglan said. "And I've decided she's not for me. I'm in a bad humor for a reason, Bart. The Vigilantes strung up old Luke Chronister last night."

That wiped the grin off Somers' face. "The hell they did!"

"I cut him down, just this morning."

"It looks as though there'll be hell to pay around these parts before long."

"Yeah, if certain hombres don't quit rustling," Raglan said. "And if they won't quit, why don't they have sense enough to lie low for a while, at least?"

"Maybe some friend should tip them off to lay off till things quiet down."

"Maybe. But a good friend should tell them to lay off for keeps."

Somers grinned. "That's a thought," he said, and moved to the door with a swagger. From the doorway, he asked, "That advice wasn't meant for me too, was it, bucko?"

Raglan said, "If the boot fits—"

Somers laughed and went out.

The counterman had been listening to the conversation, and now he said, "That Bart, there's a man who likes trouble. But one of these days he's apt to find more than he can handle."

He'd put into words what Raglan was thinking.

It was nearly sundown when Raglan reached 77 headquarters. The hands were in off the range, several just putting up their horses but most waiting around to be called to supper. Limpy Shayne was hitching up the harness-broken matched sorrels to the buckboard, and he called, "Ed, you're wanted over at the house."

Raglan nodded, off-saddled his dun, turned it into the corral, and headed for the big log-and-stone ranch house. Lyle Creighton opened the door to his knock. The ranch manager, already dressed for the party at Tomahawk, said curtly, "Come in, Ed," and crossed the hallway to his office.

It was more like a den than an office, a comfortable room reflecting the habits of a man who liked to take his ease in solitude. Here Creighton had his books, pipe, and liquor cabinet containing nothing stronger than port wine. Here he would sit at night when everyone else at 77 Ranch, including Mrs. Creighton, was abed. Raglan, who slept little and prowled much, often saw a lamp burning in the room at midnight and later. He was seldom invited into it, and now Creighton did not ask him to sit down even though Creighton seated himself at his desk.

"Ed, I hear that you caught a rustler this morning."

"Tip Nolan didn't lose any time telling you about it."

"Was it supposed to be a secret?"

Raglan shook his head. "Not at all," he said. "But I caught the rustler and I took care of him. There was no need to bother you with it."

Creighton frowned. He was ordinarily a mild-mannered man, but tonight he seemed a bit touchy. He was a transplanted Easterner who had been sent out to handle 77's business affairs two years ago, by the Crown Land & Cattle Company. He was a graying man of fifty-odd, typically a big city man. He knew nothing of cattle, but, as Raglan had found out, he was a great one for keeping the ranch accounts straight. Of late he had been a bit hard to get along with, for he was worrying that the rustlers might make such inroads on 77's herds that the ranch would fail to show a profit which would satisfy the company officials.

Creighton said, "I'm bothered when I don't know what's going on, Ed."

"I didn't say that I wouldn't have told you about that rustler, Mr. Creighton."

"Tip says you left him off with nothing more than a roughing up.'

"He won't do any more rustling on this range, sir."

"Can you be sure of that?"

"Yes. I gave him a talking to as well as a roughing up."

Creighton's frown deepened. "As I understand it, these people aren't to be reasoned with," he said.

"Mr. Creighton, I can't see hanging a man for stealing cattle."

"Nor can I, Ed. But if there's no other way to stop the stealing—"

"A man was hanged last night," Raglan said. "That will stop him from rustling, but I doubt if it will stop anybody else—not the big-time rustlers, anyway."

He watched Creighton to see if the news of a hanging surprised him at all. It seemed not to, and therefore, Raglan told himself, the man had possessed foreknowledge that Luke Chronister was slated to be the Vigilantes' latest victim. He felt sure that Creighton hadn't ridden with the others last night, however; the men who had done the hanging wouldn't have wanted a tenderfoot along. Still, it seemed to Raglan that Lyle Creighton must share some of the guilt.

"I didn't want you here to discuss the right or wrong of hanging these outlaws," Creighton said, "but to discuss your taking it on yourself to let a rustler go free once you caught him."

"That's a matter I've decided for myself. And I won't be argued out of it."

"The other ranchers won't like it."

"That's too bad."

Creighton reached for his pipe and began filling it from a pouch. "You're in a bad humor about this, Ed," he said, less curtly. "In a way, I don't blame you. I don't like violence, either, but these are violent times. Who was this rustler? Tip said he didn't know him, that he was a stranger on this range."

"Will Vance is his name."

"Where's he from?"

"I wouldn't know."

"What's his brand?"

"I doubt if he's got a brand."

Creighton looked surprised. "Then what is he brand blotting cattle for?"

Raglan shrugged. "Maybe he's getting paid for it."

"By whom?"

Raglan didn't answer.

"You won't say?"

"No. And for good reason."

Creighton stared at him, frowning again, then lighted his pipe. "So you're shielding somebody," he said. "Ed, I don't think you can get away with that. With me, maybe. But not with Matthew Dane and the others. They'll insist that you tell what you know. You'd better make up your mind to tell at Tomahawk tonight."

Raglan's face hardened. "I've been wondering why Matthew Dane should invite me to his party," he said. "I was told in town that his shindig was nothing more than a cover-up for a Vigilante meeting. From what you've just said, I'm beginning to believe it's just that. If that's so, then—you can give Mr. Dane my regrets."

He turned to leave, then faced about as Creighton said sharply, "Hold on, Ed."

The 77 manager rose, and for the first time Ed Raglan saw that there was a hard core to him. Creighton said, "You'll go to Tomahawk tonight, or you'll be without a job in the morning. Now, damn it, the choice is yours!"

CHAPTER THREE

Raglan's impulse was to tell Creighton what he could do with the job, but at that moment Mrs. Creighton appeared. He held his temper out of respect for her. She was a small, pleasant woman and always friendly toward him and the other hands. Entering the office, she pirouetted before them.

"How do I look, gentlemen?"

She knew they were angry and was deliberately trying to soothe their ruffled tempers. Like her husband, she was dressed for the Dane party. She wore an orchid dress that went well with her gray-touched hair.

Raglan smiled. "You'll be the belle of the ball, Mrs. Creighton."

She curtsied. "Thank you, kind sir. Lyle?"

Creighton's frown faded. "I agree with Ed," he told her.

She thanked him, then faced Raglan. "Of course, you're only flattering me. But you'll have to stand by your flattery. I'll expect you to dance with me at least once, Ed. Promise?"

She was so beguiling that he found himself doing as she wanted, saying that he would indeed dance with her. She patted his arm, showing that she was pleased with him for agreeing that he would come to Tomahawk in spite of his quarrel with Creighton. She was more of a diplomat than her husband.

But he was a little annoyed with himself for having given in to her. He left the house, still not wanting to attend a Vigilante meeting. The other hands, were at supper in the cook shack and the bunkhouse was empty. He got his dress-up clothes from his warsack, found a bar of yellow soap, and went downstream of the creek. There, screened by a big willow tree, he stripped and took a bath. He dressed, trying to shake the wrinkles from his seldom worn gray broadcloth suit before donning it, then returned to the bunkhouse where he combed his hair and finally examined himself in the foggy wall mirror. Tip Nolan entered, forcing a grin that had little amusement in it.

"You look right handsome," Tip said. "You'll have to fight off the women."

"That I'll have to see."

"Just don't get gay with Matt Dane's daughter."

"I'll watch my step," Raglan said, and picked up his hat from his bunk and went out.

The Creightons had already left in the buckboard, so he went to the corral and roped and saddled a mount, a gray from his string, and set out for Tomahawk. There was a trace of road running across the dozen miles between the two ranch headquarters, the last half mile winding through a range of low hills. He overtook the Creightons in the hills, and followed the buckboard through to the head, of the small valley in which Matthew Dane had located his buildings.

Dane was a big man, and he'd built big. His buildings were numerous and solidly constructed of log on stone foundations. The main house was twice the size of the 77 ranchhouse, and tonight its front doorway and many windows glowed with lamplight. Music and voices came from the house. The far end of the yard, over by the barn and corrals, was filled with rigs—buggies, buckboards, carriages. A Tomahawk hand was on hand to take the Creighton rig. Raglan rode to the corrals and put up his own mount.

There were so many guests that some had overflowed onto the porch which ran the length of the house. Matthew Dane, a red-faced bull of a man, stood there talking to the Creightons. Like most of the cattlemen on the range, he had moved his outfit up from Texas when Wyoming and Montana were opened to stock raising. Dane had been the first to settle in Tulare Basin, and for the first year or two he had tried to control the whole of that vast range. Finally the other outfits had broken his control through sheer weight of numbers, and, Raglan had an idea, that defeat still rankled in the man.

He turned as Raglan mounted the stone steps, offering his hand and saying in his bellowing voice, "Welcome to Tomahawk, Ed. Have yourself a time. It's my daughter's twentieth birthday, and I want it to be one she'll remember!"

Shaking hands with him, Raglan wondered how sincere the man's welcome really was. He couldn't believe that Dane had forgotten that they'd once fallen out over Laurie, but he read nothing in that heavy red face. Matthew Dane was a poker player, and what went on in his mind was his own secret.

Raglan said, "I'll have to congratulate your daughter."

"Do that. You'll find her around. If you're hungry or thirsty, you'll find a table loaded with grub and liquid refreshments. We're having what Laurie calls a buffet supper." He winked at Raglan. "She's trying to rub off some of her expensive education onto the old man."

He turned back to the Creightons and Raglan went inside, looking for Laurie.

Music was furnished by two fiddlers and a banjoist, and a portion of the enormous parlor had been cleared of furniture and rugs to permit dancing. Laurie was whirling about with young Clay Mowbrey, son of the owner of Slash M. A fine looking blonde girl with lively blue eyes and a bright smile, she saw Raglan as Clay executed a turn and her smile widened and a glow came into her eyes. Ed nodded, returning the smile.

He saw Clara Amberton, Frank's wife, sweep by in the arms of Jess Owens, foreman of the Running W, and noted, among the thirty or more people in the room, several ramrods from other outfits. This was significant, for Matthew Dane didn't make a habit of mingling socially with hired hands. Ed watched both Laurie Dane and Clara Amberton for a moment, thinking how the two of them had touched briefly on his life and then passed him by. Clara had married Frank, and Laurie, much too young, had been sent East so she would get over her crush on him.

Both were attractive, and Raglan found himself wondering idly why neither had become important to him—or he to them. The half-formed idea came to him that a man without a woman of his own was not a complete man, and he looked at the dark-haired Clara and felt that Frank Amberton was a lucky man. He studied Laurie and wondered what it would be like to have such a girl for a wife. She was no longer a flighty half-child, half-woman as she'd been three years ago. She had blossomed into a fine maturity.

He saw Frank Amberton at the far end of the room, at the punch bowl on the huge laden table. He circled the dancing couples, made his way to Amberton and picked up a glass.

"This lemonade spiked with anything, Frank?"

"Hardly, with ladies present."

"I noticed Clara when I came in. She grows prettier all the while."

"Tell her so. She'll be pleased."

Raglan filled his glass with lemonade. "I'll do that, now that I have your permission." He lifted his glass to Amberton. "Mud in your eye, bucko."

Amberton smiled, and for a moment they were close again. They'd ridden together on many a roundup in their Texas days. Amberton was a darkly handsome man, but stocky. He was growing a little thick about the middle, Raglan noted, and a hint of pudgy softness blurred his features. He was as neatly dressed as a prosperous townsman, and maybe he had all but forgotten his cowhand days.

After a sip of lemonade Raglan said, low-voiced, "I ran into Will Vance this morning."

"Vance? Somebody I know?"

"Let's not play games, Frank. He's somebody you know, all right."

Amberton set down his glass, took out and lighted a cigar. "All right, Ed," he said. "Let's not play games. You ran into Will Vance, and I know a man by that name. So?"

"He was changing a Seventy-seven on a yearling into a Ladder A," Raglan said. "We had a little argument about it, and Vance gave me his word that he wouldn't get caught at that sort of thing again on this range."

Amberton appeared casual enough, puffing on his cigar. But there was a trace of worry in his eyes. "Who was with you when you caught him at it, Ed?"

"A Seventy-seven cowhand."

"Will he keep his mouth shut?"

"He didn't see what brand Vance was changing that Seventy-seven to. And I didn't tell him. But aren't you asking whether or not I'll keep my mouth shut?"

The worry faded from Amberton's eyes. "You will," he said. "For old times' sake. Or if not for that, for Clara's sake. Feeling as you do about her, or as you once felt, you wouldn't want to make trouble."

"How many more riders like Vance have you got, Frank?"

"I've got half a dozen maverickers. But you know how such men are. They work until they've got a few dollars ahead and then lay off until it's spent."

"Get rid of them."

"That sounds like an order, Ed."

"Call it what you like. Just get rid of them."

"I have as much right to get a share of the mavericks as any-body else."

"I'm talking about the brand blotting they're doing."

Amberton puffed on his cigar, smiling and shaking his head. "You've made a mistake, Ed. Nobody's doing any brand blotting for me. Why, that's something I don't approve of. You know that."

Raglan emptied his glass. The lemonade tasted sour. "It's not what I know that counts. It's what somebody else is going to find out. What do you think would happen if Matt Dane discovered that you're a damn rustler?"

The music stopped. Laurie left her partner and came hurrying to Raglan. She linked arms with him, bubbling with laughter.

"Ed, darling!" she exclaimed. "What a nice birthday present!"

"Congratulations, Laurie. Many happy returns of the day."

"Thanks. Seeing my old flame makes it perfect."

"Got a new flame now?"

Before Laurie could answer, Frank Amberton said, "We'll talk again, Ed. More in earnest, eh?" He moved away.

Laurie hugged Raglan's arm. "It's good to see you again, Ed," she said, lowering her voice. "But seeing you here is a surprise. I didn't think Dad would ever let you darken his door."

"Well, he did. For reasons of his own, I suppose. But you didn't answer me."

"What did you ask me?"

"Are you still rattle-brained, child?"

"Rattle-brained, but no longer a child. Let's go out for a breath of air."

They walked out to the porch, passing her father and the Creightons in the hall. Matthew Dane maintained his poker face at seeing them together. They walked to the far end of the porch, and Laurie perched prettily on the peeled log railing.

"You asked me if I've got a new flame now," she said. "You see? I'm not rattle-brained. But what if I have a beau? Would you be jealous?"

"How should I know?"

"Now don't answer a question with a question."

"Don't you, either."

They laughed together, and Raglan found himself liking this girl. He had to remind himself that she was not for him. Her father would have other plans for her, not marriage with a mere ranch foreman.

Laurie grew grave and watched him for a time without speaking. He busied himself with rolling and lighting a cigarette. He found her pleasant company yet something was missing. If desire lurked in him, it was merely a smoldering thing and Laurie didn't fan the embers into flame. He felt merely lukewarm toward her, as he had toward Clara before she married Frank Amberton. He wondered what ailed him. He was, now that he analyzed himself, one of the loneliest of men. He needed a woman in his life and it seemed that the blame must lie with him that he didn't desire Laurie Dane. She was attractive enough, and more.

She said, "Still my friend, Ed?"

"Why, sure."

"Do something for me?"

"If it won't make trouble between me and your father."

"He needn't know."

He regarded her doubtfully. Three years ago an escapade of hers had made him and Matthew Dane enemies—not violent foes, but still enemies. She had come riding out to his place on Squaw Creek, and Dane, learning of her visit, had suspected the worst. Outraged, the man had accused Raglan of seducing his daughter. There'd been a moment when it seemed that Dane would grab for his gun, but it ended with the cattleman ordering Raglan to leave Tulare Basin, and with Raglan defying him and telling him to keep his daughter at home. Laurie finally convinced her father that Raglan had not taken advantage of her at all, but Matthew Dane had never forgiven the younger man for his defiance. If she now planned to put something over on her father, who was not easily fooled, it proved that Laurie hadn't learned her lesson three years ago. Raglan shied away from her, mentally.

But curiosity made him ask, "What do you want, Laurie?"

She glanced past him, making sure none of the other guests was close enough to overhear. Then: "You know Bart Somers who used to work here at Tomahawk?"

He nodded.

Laurie asked, "Could you get in touch with him for me?"

"Maybe. I saw him only today, in Bennett," Raglan said. "Where he'd be now, I wouldn't know."

"He has friends over in the Hatchet Hills. The Mallorys."

Raglan thought of the girl, Christine. He said, "Maybe they'd tell me where to find him—if I decide to get in touch with him. What's this all about, anyway?"

"Bart and I—well, we got to be friendly when he was at Tomahawk."

"Ah?"

"He's nice," Laurie said, defensively. "He's a lot of fun."

"I'll bet. And not half so slow about making the most of his opportunities as I was three years ago."

"Don't be jealous, Ed. You're not in love with me. Don't think you are."

He smiled. "All right. If I get in touch with Bart, what then?"

"Tell him I said he's to be careful," Laurie said gravely. "Tell him the Vigilantes know that he's a rustler and have him on their list." She laid a hand on his arm. "Will you do that, Ed?"

"How do you know his name's on the Vigilantes' list?"

"I overheard Dad and Frank Amberton talking."

"You're sure they're after him because he's a rustler?"

"Of course. Why else would Dad have said he's on the list?"

"Maybe because he's found out that you and Bart are friendly."

Laurie considered that, frowning. "No, that couldn't be," she said. "I've only seen Bart once since he left Tomahawk, and that was about three months ago. Besides, if my father knew about it and objected, he wouldn't have the Vigilantes go after Bart. He'd take care of it himself."

Raglan didn't argue the point, but he wasn't so sure that Matthew Dane would handle the matter personally if he objected to Laurie having an affair with Bart Somers. Which he certainly would, when he found out. That was one of the reasons for Raglan's violent disapproval of men banding together as vigilantes: always, some members used the organization to work off personal grudges or for grinding personal axes.

He said, "I'll give Bart your message if I run into him."

"And you'll really try to find him?"

"I suppose so," Raglan said.

She squeezed his arm by way of thanks, then got down from her perch on the railing as young Clay Mowbrey came searching for her. The youth looked a bit sulky over finding her with Raglan; quite obviously he had lost his heart over Laurie Dane. Watching them go off together, Raglan wondered if Matthew Dane approved of young Mowbrey as a suitor for his daughter. Then he began thinking about what he'd promised the girl. He didn't doubt for a moment that he would keep the promise.

Indeed, he looked forward to keeping it. By inquiring for Bart Somers at the Mallory place, he would almost certainly see Christine again.

Odd, that. His reunion with Laurie served only to make him think of the Mallory girl ....

CHAPTER FOUR

H e stayed at the end of the porch for some little while, feeling somehow that he didn't fit in here even though he knew almost everyone present. Guest or not, he was just a hired hand while most of the other men were ranch owners or highly paid representatives of owner-companies. For the first time since taking the job as foreman of 77 Ranch, he wished he had remained a two-bit rancher, and he knew a sudden homesickness for his cabin on Squaw Creek.

He supposed he felt that way because of his quarrel with Lyle Creighton. But also he suspected that a man was better off as his own boss, even though it meant a struggle, than to be somebody else's man. He'd hired on with 77 because Creighton had offered him seventy-five dollars a month, good pay for a man with only a couple of hundred head of cattle in his own brand, opportunity for a man who saw little hope of prosperity in being a raggedy-pants cowman.

That's how Matthew Dane had once described him. Not to his face, but jokingly to others who had told him about it. Dane had commented that Raglan's RAG brand was a fit brand for a raggedy-pants cowman, sneering at the poverty of all the small ranchers. It occurred to Raglan that the man not only was contemptuous of the ranchers who failed to prosper, but hated them as well. The thought made him wonder if Dane might not be utilizing the Vigilante movement to rid the range of the little cowmen. Certainly, the Vigilantes had gotten rid of one—Luke Chronister.

He saw Clara Amberton come onto the porch and turn in his direction. He threw away his cigarette and smiled. There was nothing flighty in Clara's nature as there was in Laurie Dane's. Clara was older, twenty-seven or eight, and wise enough to know exactly what she wanted out of life. He as well as Frank Amberton had courted her, but she had chosen Frank for a very good reason. She and Frank were both ambitious, and Frank had lifted himself above the sorry state of being a raggedy-pants cowman. Clara was tall, darkly pretty, with a full-blown figure. She had been Frank's wife for more than three years, but still there were no children. It was difficult for Raglan to imagine Clara as a mother. Indeed, he suspected that as a wife she might be a cool proposition.

But she seemed warm enough now, smiling and saying, "Off by yourself, Ed? You're like that too much of the time."

"It's a fault, Clara?"

"Women think it's a fault in an attractive man."

"I'm clumsy with women."

She shook her head. "I know you better than all that," she said, laughing. "You made love to me a time or two, and quite expertly. It's just that you lose interest when you reach a certain point. Why, Ed?"

"Maybe I'm a misfit."

"Not you. You're more virile than most men." She studied him. "I think you're the sort who needs some one certain woman. Who will it be? It wasn't I, and I don't think it's Laurie. Where will you ever find the special woman, Ed?"

"I don't know, Clara. I'll just have to keep looking."

"It will be pretty wonderful for you and the girl you find one day, Ed. Different from what it is for most couples."

"Is that so, Clara?"

She pouted wryly. "A time or two when you and I were friendly I wished that you found me special. But you never did."

"You did well enough, in Frank."

"I did, didn't I?" she said. "Why don't you come to Ladder A to dinner on Sunday? It's been more than a year since you visited us. We'll have so much to talk about, you and Frank and I."

He knew then: Frank had sent her to talk to him, so he'd be reminded that he'd once thought a great deal of Clara. Frank was making sure that Ed Raglan would keep his mouth shut about the brand blotting Will Vance had done.

"Will you come Sunday, Ed?"

"Yes," he said. "Thanks."

Clara had just left him when Lyle Creighton appeared. He beat about the bush for a moment, asking Raglan if he were enjoying himself and if he'd had some refreshments. Then, a bit edgily, he said, "I'd like you to come along over to the barn, Ed."

"So the meeting is about to be called to order, eh?"

"Dane wanted it, Ed. I couldn't refuse to come, or refuse to bring you."

"I'm here," Raglan said. "I'll see it through."

They left the porch, crossed the ranchyard. The barn was lighted by a couple of lanterns, and the other male guests already had gathered inside with their host. Raglan counted twenty-four men, five besides himself being ranch foremen. Matthew Dane took the floor, arrogant and loud.

"Gentlemen, you all know there's a Vigilante group active on this range," he began. "I've been asked to speak to you on behalf of this group, the members of which must go unknown here and elsewhere.

"You all know, too, that the rustling in Tulare Basin has gotten out of hand. We've got more thieves on this range than honest men, and there's no law—except a deputy sheriff at Bennett who may or may not be in league with the rustler element—within a hundred miles of here. Sure, we can send word to the county seat and get the sheriff out here, as we've done before, but that would gain us absolutely nothing. The sheriff doesn't know this country nor the people, and the thieves put on honest faces when he's about."

He paused to take a puff on his cigar. Then he continued, "What I'm supposed to say is that we've got to kill our own wolves. Some of the nester ranchers are rustlers, and the rest are friendly toward the rustlers—aiding and abetting them. There's evidence that some of the ranch hands in the employ of some of the big outfits are rustlers or partners with rustlers. That's why I've asked the outfits hiring ranch foremen to have their ramrods here tonight. I'd like to say to them that they've got to keep a close watch on any suspicious members of their crews. The owners bossing their own crews don't need to be told that, of course."

He puffed again on his cigar.

"Last night a man named Chronister was hanged by the Vigilantes. Evidence pointing to him as a rustler was damning, to say the least. It was gathered by a range detective in the employ of the Tulare Basin Cattlemen's Association, to which most of us here belong. Now, friends, I'm told that only this morning the foreman of Seventy-seven Ranch caught a rustler at work with a running iron."

He looked at Ed Raglan, his manner suddenly challenging.

They all looked at Raglan. All but Frank Amberton, he noticed.

Dane said, "Ed, I think I can speak for all of us here. We'd like to know about this rustler you caught."

"Didn't Mr. Creighton tell you about it, Matt?" He saw Dane's frown, and knew the man resented being addressed so familiarly by a mere ranch foreman. "It wasn't much. I caught him with a Seventy-seven yearling, working its brand over."

"Well, who was the man?"

"Will Vance."

"Where's he hang out?"

"I don't know that."

Dane turned to the others. "Anybody know about this Vance?"

Nobody answered, but Frank Amberton smiled faintly. If he was worried that Raglan would let the truth out, he did not show it.

"What's his brand?" Dane asked, swinging back.

"Like I told Mr. Creighton, I don't know if he has a brand of his own."

"Well, what was he changing Seventy-seven's brand into?"

"I've forgotten, if I ever knew."

"You shielding some raggedy-pants cowman, Ed?"

Raglan looked him straight in the eye. "No."

"Then why this lapse of memory?"

Raglan shrugged.

A heavy silence grew in the barn for a lengthy interval. Then Hank Mockridge, one of two brothers owning the Double M outfit, said sourly, "Talking about raggedy-pants cowmen, I understand Raglan is one himself, along with being foreman for Seventy-seven."

Raglan said, "What's that supposed to prove, Hank?"

"Nothing, maybe. Or everything."

"If you want to call me a rustler, go ahead. But get some proof of it first. Sure, I was a raggedy-pants cowman. I had a cabin on Squaw Creek and a couple hundred head of cattle on the range— two years ago. I haven't even bothered to brand my own calf crop since then, and no man here can say he ever saw me branding with anything but a Seventy-seven during that time. What happened to my calves? Maybe some of you gentlemen know. You all go in for mavericking."

"We're not talking about mavericking," Dane said, taking it away from Mockridge. "We're discussing rustling—which is robbing us all blind."

"All right," Raglan said. "Go ahead and discuss it. Just don't go pointing an accusing finger at me."

"But you've got to admit you asked for it, man. You let Vance get away."

"I roughed him up. I warned him not to let me catch him again." Raglan's temper was slipping, his voice increasingly harsh. "I don't think he'll do any more brand changing on this range. In fact, I'd bet a month's wages on it. If you want him hanged like Luke Chronister, you'll have to do the job. Me, I'm not a hangman—legal or otherwise."

Matthew Dane's poker face broke. His countenance was beet red and stiff with rage. "Damn it, Ed," he said, almost shouting, "you've refused to tell us what brand Vance burned on that Seventy-seven cow. You've refused to tell your own boss, Lyle Creighton. What are we to think of you, anyway?"

"Think what you like," Raglan said. "I was invited to a party. Now it turns out to be a Vigilante meeting. I don't belong here. I'm not a Vigilante."

He strode to the doorway, paused there, and said savagely, "While you're thinking, you might think about this. Maybe I'm shielding someone here when I cover up what Vance was doing with his running iron. Maybe I'm shielding one of you honest-faced gentlemen. Now good night to the lot of you!"

He had a glimpse of Frank Amberton's face as he turned away, and the man appeared jolted to the core. But the others were gripped by shock, too. He didn't hear a sound behind him as he went to the corral to get his horse, and when he rode out, minutes later, there was only an uncertain muttering of voices in the barn. To hell with them, he thought.

Leaving the Tomahawk ranchyard, he felt angry with himself for having blurted out that he was shielding one of the group. Still, on the other hand, Frank Amberton was in need of a scare. Maybe this would serve as one, a scare sufficient to make him quit making deals with men like Will Vance to change other outfits' brands to his Ladder A.

On that thought he lifted his gray to a lope, and headed for 77 Ranch.

Where, he reflected, Lyle Creighton would fire him in the morning ....

CHAPTER FIVE

He waited around after sending the hands out onto the range. When Creighton appeared, around nine o'clock, he was at the blacksmith shed shoeing a horse. He let the manager stand around while he finished with the horse, then put away the tools, removed the leather apron, and built a smoke. By now Creighton was seated on an empty horseshoe keg, smoking a cigar.

He said, "Ed, you sure set off a bomb in Tomahawk's barn last night."

The friendliness of his voice surprised Raglan. He'd expected the man to be sore, to raise Cain and then fire him. "I guess I did, at that," he said.

"Saying that you were covering up for someone in that group made them forget about the other rustlers. Everybody was suspicious of everybody else, and the meeting got out of hand for Matt Dane."

"And now he's got more reason for hating, my guts."

"He tried to tell the others you'd lied, but he quit that in a hurry because it made him look suspicious. Hank Mockridge pointed out to him that so far as anybody knew you were a man of your word."

"Well, I told them the truth."

"I won't ask you to tell me whom you're shielding," Creighton said. "But the problem is this, Ed. I'm supposed to look out for Seventy-seven's interests to the best of my ability. I'm not doing my job if I let Seventy-seven stock continue to be stolen. Now, what are we going to do about this rustler who's posing as a respectable rancher?"

"He's had a scare thrown into him," Raglan said. "That should be enough to make him play the game straight from now on. If it isn't, I'll give him a warning the next time we catch one of his men blotting brands."

Creighton nodded. "I'll go along with that. But if the scare and a warning don't stop him, some action will have to be taken."

"It won't go that far. Our man isn't that much a fool."

"I suppose not. Now what about the matter Dane brought up last night?"

"About some of the hands working for the big outfits being rustlers?"

"Yes. Do you think it's a likelihood?"

Raglan nodded. "I know it is," he said. "The outfits offer their riders five dollars for every maverick branded. At first, that seems like a lot of easy money. But after a while some cowpuncher or other gets the notion that if it's worth five dollars for him to put a maverick in his outfit's brand, it would be worth five or six times as much if he put it in a brand of his own."

He paused to flip away his cigarette. "So he dreams up a brand for himself and burns it on an occasional maverick—with an eye to the future. He figures that in a few years he'll be a cattleman on his own. But there's so many men mavericking nowadays that mavericks are becoming few and far between. And it's mighty easy to use a running iron on a cow already carrying a brand."

"Any men in our crew pulling that?"

"No. I watch them too close." Raglan kicked his heel into the dirt. "Maybe I'd better not say that. I could be fooled. Some of these riders are pretty tricky. Besides, like Matt Dane said, they could be partners with rustlers not working for any outfit. They could throw a few head of cattle into some lonely spot for their friends to brand. Anything is possible on open range." He gave Creighton an amused look. "I'll keep a closer watch on our hands, if I'm still on the payroll."

Creighton laughed. "Did you really think you'd lose your job because of what happened last night?"

"The thought did occur to me," Raglan said.

He rode out a few minutes later, heading toward the Hatchet Hills. Three hours later he entered the little valley where Luke Chronister had lived. He rode by the deserted buildings, and saw the new grave near the cottonwood tree where the man had been hanged. There was a pine-board marker at the head of the grave, and someone had used a running iron to burn this legend into the marker:

Luke Chronister
Murdered by Vigilantes—Aug. 13th, 1885
RIP

Raglan shook his head frowningly, then turned away across the valley. Minutes later he rode through the gap in the low hills and entered another small valley. A ranch headquarters was located at the far end, and he aimed directly toward it.

There was the usual barn, a couple of sheds, and an L-shaped house. Half a dozen chickens scratched around in the yard, while a dog lay in the shade of one shed and, too lazy to get up, barked at Raglan in a halfhearted fashion. The place had the poverty-stricken appearance of all two-bit ranches, but Raglan saw no litter about the buildings. This showed a woman's touch, he told himself. Christine Mallory was a good housekeeper. It must be Christine who kept things tidy, because he'd heard that her mother had died long before the family came to Wyoming from the Brazos River country of Texas.

A man stepped from the barn and watched Raglan ride in, at the same time scattering a handful of grain for the chickens which fluttered about him with a great squawking. He was a gaunt man of about sixty with a short iron-gray beard. At first glance he appeared frail because of his age and leanness. Then Raglan saw the leathery skin and the stringy-muscled body and realized that here was a man hardy enough to stand the rigors of life as a nester rancher. Reining in, he noted the brightness of the man's eyes. Sam Mallory—this must be Sam Mallory—also possessed a still youthful spirit.

He said, "Mr. Mallory?"

"I'm Sam Mallory." He smiled. "Though I'm seldom called *Mister* Mallory."

"I'm Ed Raglan from over at Seventy-seven Ranch."

Mallory nodded. "What can I do for you, Raglan?"

A movement over at the house caught Raglan's attention. He looked that way and saw Christine at the door. He was aware of a quickening of his pulse, and he knew that this was what he had wanted: a glimpse of her. He lifted his hat. She gave him the briefest of nods. He turned back to her father.

"There is something you may be able to do for me, Mr. Mallory," he said. "I'm looking for Bart Somers. Maybe you can help me get in touch with him."

"Why me?"

"I was told that he has some friends named Mallory."

"Oh?"

"The only Mallorys I know of live here in the Hatchets."

Sam Mallory shook his head. "In these times a man can't just ride up to a place and ask folks to help him find a man they may or may not know."

"I'm aware of that," Raglan told him. "But I have a message for Somers, from a good friend of his. The message is important."

"Maybe Somers ain't interested."

"That could be. Still, I'd like to deliver the message."

Mallory glanced past Raglan to his daughter. He nodded to her, then said, "Dinner's on the table. My boys are off somewhere and won't be here to eat. There should be enough for you. Come along, Raglan."

"Well—thanks."

He dismounted, left his horse ground-hitched in the shade at the side of the barn. He followed Mallory around the rear of the house, to the nearby creek. They washed their hands, then went into the kitchen where Christine was setting another place at the table.

Mallory said, "You've met my daughter, eh, Raglan?"

"Yes, sir." Raglan grinned at the girl. "I hope I'm not putting you to a lot of bother."

"There's a place set for you."

She averted her eyes and began putting the meal on the table.

Mallory chuckled. "Some folks don't like visitors from the big outfits. Chris is one." He turned solemn the next instant. "She told me you cut Luke down. I tried to explain to her that if you'd had a hand in what happened to him you wouldn't have showed up there that morning. Unless—" he gave Raglan a searching look—"you've got a queer sort of mind."

"I didn't know Chronister was dead until I saw him hanging there," Raglan said. "More than that, I never had any idea that he was suspected of being a rustler."

Sam Mallory seemed to take his word for that, but Chris's manner remained aloof and chill. No more was said about Luke Chronister's death. In fact, there was no conversation at all during the meal. Like most cow country folks, the Mallorys came to the table to eat, not to talk. When they had finished, and left the table, Raglan complimented Christine on her cooking.

She replied frigidly, "I'm glad you enjoyed it."

They got their hats and went outside, hunkering down in the shade of the trees along the creek. Raglan rolled a cigarette and Mallory filled his pipe. They smoked a little while in silence.

Mallory said, "About Bart Somers. You've really got a message for him?"

"That's right. From a friend, as I told you."

"I haven't seen him for two, three weeks. He comes by here once in a while." He nodded toward the house. "Because of Chris. He'd come oftener if she'd encourage him. My two boys, Jess and Steve, they went on hunting trips with him two, three times. They may know how to get in touch with him."

"When will they be home, Sam?"

"Can't say. Maybe late tonight. Maybe tomorrow. Maybe the next day."

Raglan nodded and did not inquire into the prowlings of the Mallory boys. After a lengthy silence, he said, "Well, I can't wait around, that's sure. I've got no business being away from Seventy-seven range now."

"If I can get word to Somers, I'll tell him to get in touch with you."

"That wouldn't do."

"No?"

Raglan rubbed his cigarette into the dirt. Then he said, "Sam, I'm going to give you the message for him. I have a notion you won't repeat it to anybody else. If it got out that I carried it, I'd be in a jam—and so would Somers's friend." He waited, but Mallory silently puffed on his pipe. He went on, "The message is, he's to be careful because his name is on the Vigilantes' list."

Sam Mallory's face remained expressionless, but there was a tightness to his voice as he said, "All right."

Raglan rose. "I'll be moving along. Thanks for dinner."

"Come again, when you can."

"Thanks."

He stopped at the kitchen door to say good-by to Christine. She turned from washing the dishes, drying her hands on her apron. Her manner was no friendlier than it had been during dinner.

"A word of advice, Raglan," she said. "My brothers aren't as easy-going as my father. They don't take to big-outfit men any more than I do. I wouldn't come here again, if I were you."

"I was figuring on dropping by some Sunday afternoon, to sit with you."

"You're not keeping company with me, Raglan."

"Sunday after next, maybe."

"I told you—"

"So long until then, Chris," he said quickly, and turned away.

Riding from the Mallory place, he had to face it: he was smitten. But having fallen for Christine was apt to get him no more than a hard time. He had to admit that too. In her eyes, he was a big-outfit man and for her that was reason enough to hate him. Somehow, he would have to overcome her prejudice. That somehow wouldn't be easily hit upon, but he felt a pleasant glow regardless. He knew now why Clara Amberton, nee Hendricks, and Laurie Dane had never been too important for him. He'd been waiting for Christine Mallory, a girl he hadn't met.

Still thinking about Christine he crossed the dead Luke Chronister's little valley. He was completely off guard when the rifle cracked.

The shriek of the slug told him he was the target. He jerked his sorrel gelding to a rearing halt, grabbed his rifle from its boot and flung himself from the saddle. The second shot came as he dropped to the ground. He heard the slug strike the horse, dropping it in its tracks. The animal, hit in the head, died almost instantly. A third slug kicked dirt into Raglan's face. He swore, partly with anger and partly with alarm, and cast about frantically for cover.

He lay midway between the cottonwood where Luke Chronister had been hanged, and the dead man's log buildings. The cabin or barn would give him better cover, but the ambusher would expect him to head for the buildings and might be thrown off if he turned back toward the tree. He heaved over in a quick roll, came to his feet and began to run. He'd guessed right. The next shot did not come until he reached the cottonwood, and then it went far wide of him. He crouched by the thick trunk of the tree, levered a cartridge into the Winchester's chamber, peered at the slope from which the shots had come.

A profusion of scrub pines fanned up the slope and extended over its crest, and the bushwhacker was screened by them. Raglan waited, peering upward until his eyes ached, but saw nothing of his man.

His first flash of fear had faded. He felt steadier. He began to wonder about this attempt on his life, and his first thought was: *Sam Mallory?*

It would have been possible for Mallory to take a short cut through the hills, he supposed, but, having eaten at the man's table and talked with him, he couldn't figure Mallory as a man who'd kill from ambush. It occurred to him that the man on the slope might be another friend of Luke Chronister who had seen him crossing the valley and decided to avenge Chronister's death by killing him, a big-outfit man. But that seemed unlikely, because there was no reason for one of the dead man's friends to be on the slope to begin with. Raglan discarded the idea.

There was another possibility. The gunman might have followed him into the hills from Seventy-seven range. Raglan found himself thinking, That has to be the explanation, and it filled him with dread. It meant that even if he killed or drove off the ambusher, the danger would not be ended for him. It meant that he was a marked man.

Why?

He knew the answer even as the question came into his mind. He had thrown a scare into somebody with his outburst in the Tomahawk barn last night; such a scare that the somebody—Frank Amberton—felt that he was too much of a threat to let live.

Frank Amberton, his old friend .... But it wouldn't be Frank up there on the slope with a hot rifle in his hands and murder in his heart. Frank had never been any good with a gun. In fact, he was one of the few men on the range who seldom carried a six-shooter or a rifle. If Amberton wanted him dead, then the bushwhacker was somebody in his hire.

Even as Raglan told himself that, his mind tried to reject the idea. They'd been friends, and Amberton must know that friendship would keep him silent about the brand blotting for Ladder A. Besides, the man had never been a vicious sort .... Still, he hadn't imagined that Amberton would turn to stealing. If ambition had made Frank greedy, and greed had made him a thief, then it might be possible that Frank Amberton was capable of having murder done.

Raglan shook his head, his troubled gaze still searching the slope. He had an enemy in Matthew Dane, he told himself. Maybe Dane had gotten a bellyful of him last night and put somebody on his trail. The Tomahawk owner had plenty of gunmen in his crew. Then there was Will Vance whom he'd roughed up. The brand blotter might have more spirit than Raglan had seen in him, and might be trying to work off a grudge. Raglan didn't know what to think.

It was somebody with plenty of nerve, he had to admit, for now the bushwhacker opened up on him again, firing three rapid shots and putting the slugs close enough to make him flinch. He had the rifleman's position marked now, by the powdersmoke from the shots, and he drove two shots into the scrub pines shrouded by the smoke. He waited a moment, then fired twice more when there was no answering shot from the slope. He found no target, but at least he flushed his man. He saw a movement among the trees, then made out the shape of the fleeing man. He fired again until his rifle was empty, still missing. The bushwhacker continued his flight while Raglan reloaded his Winchester, crossing a bare spot near the crest of the slope. The distance was too great for Raglan to get a good look at his quarry, and the next instant the man vanished into a dense thicket. A moment later he was in the saddle and riding south along the ridge at a lope, shortly disappearing and leaving Raglan feeling relieved but still mystified.

Pursuit was out of the question, so Raglan sank to a sitting position, his back to the tree trunk and his rifle across his knees, and took out makings. He smoked for a while, thinking about the attempt on his life and worrying about it. He was certain of only one angle of the ugly business: the gunman had definitely come from outside the Hatchets and therefore was not somebody trying to avenge Luke Chronister's death by killing a big-outfit man. But if it had been Will Vance or one of Matthew Dane's tough hands or somebody sent by Frank Amberton, he did not know. He could take it for granted, however, that the bushwhacking, having failed, wouldn't be the last try at him. He would have to watch his step every minute from now on, and his danger was all the greater for his not knowing the identity of his would-be killer.

He rose when his cigarette was smoked short, and stripped the rigging off his dead horse. He booted his rifle, tied bridle and saddle blanket behind the cantle, and heaved the saddle onto his shoulder. The dozen miles to Seventy-seven headquarters promised too long a hike, so he turned in the direction of the Mallory ranch.

CHAPTER SIX

It was farther to the Mallory place than he'd realized from riding there earlier. His cowpuncher boots hadn't been built for walking and they pinched badly by the time he reached the ranchyard. Sam Mallory watched him come in, from over by the corral, and Christine stood at her kitchen door. Curiosity got the better of her and she came to hear what he had to say. He dumped his saddle, and grinned ruefully at the old man.

"Got set afoot over by Chronister's place," he said. "Could you loan me a mount?"

"Sure. Squat and rest. I'll drop my loop on a bronc."

"It was somebody with a rifle who set me afoot."

"Somebody from the Hatchets?"

"No. Somebody from outside."

"Why?" It was Christine who asked. "Why did somebody from outside shoot your horse?"

"He was aiming at me," Raglan told her. "The range was just long enough to throw off his aim a few inches."

They stared at him, Mallory wonderingly and Christine with suspicion.

Mallory said, "Somebody tried to kill you because you carried a message to Bart Somers?"

Raglan shook his head. "Not that. I talked out of turn last night at a party at Tomahawk. I made an enemy of somebody. I don't know just who, yet."

He removed his hat and used his shirt sleeve to wipe sweat from his forehead. He hunkered down in the shade of the barn. Mallory got a rope and went into the corral. Christine stood there watching him, frowning.

He said, "No matter what you think, I didn't shoot that horse so I had an excuse to see you again. I wouldn't go quite that far."

"Very funny," Christine said.

"Still, I'd hoof it that far to see you any day."

"Flattery won't make me like you any better, Raglan."

He sobered. "No, I guess it won't." He quit looking at her but she didn't move away.

After a moment she said, "What do you mean 'you talked out of turn'?"

"It wouldn't interest you."

"That's right. It wouldn't." She still didn't return to the house. "A party, you said?"

He nodded.

"A fancy party, like money folks throw?"

"I guess it was, sort of."

"Music and dancing?"

He looked up at her again, and saw a handsome girl in a faded calico dress. He thought of how stylishly Clara Amberton and Laurie Dane had been dressed last night, they and the other women at the party. Christine probably had no fancy clothes. But she should have, for she was a real beauty. He tried to imagine her, a back country girl at such a shindig. She would have been what he'd jokingly said Mrs. Creighton would be, the belle of the ball. She seemed a little resentful of the party at Tomahawk, a bit envious of the people who'd been there. At the same time he sensed her wistfulness. Christine too would like parties. Her life was barren of gaiety.

He said, "Music and dancing. Plenty of refreshments. I didn't have much fun."

She took that up, saying, "You had a fall-out with somebody. It must have been because of a woman. Was it?"

"You think somebody wants to kill me because of a woman?"

"Such things happen, I've heard. Especially, among money folks." She watched him closely, trying to read what she wanted to know in his expression. She was afire with curiosity. "Who is the woman—Laurie Dane?"

"You know Laurie?"

"I've seen her a couple times in Bennett."

"I didn't fall out over her with anybody."

"She's beautiful, isn't she?"

"Yeah," Raglan said, holding back a smile as he rose to go saddle the strawberry roan Sam Mallory brought from the corral.

They stood watching while he saddled the roan, the girl's gaze far more interested than her father's. Raglan was a bit amused by her. He wanted her interested in him, and he had what he wanted. The more she believed him to be friendly with Laurie Dane, the more she considered him a gay dog with the ladies, the greater her interest would become. Or so he hoped. He swung into the saddle and held the roan quiet.

"I'll return this bronc as soon as I can, if you need it," he told Mallory. "If you're in no hurry, I'll wait until Sunday a week when I come calling on your daughter."

Mallory grinned through his beard. "No hurry, Raglan."

Christine said, "Sunday a week I'll be visiting neighbors back through the hills. If the boys are here, they'll probably run you off. If they're not, you and Pa can sit and chew the fat."

Raglan laughed. "See you," he said and turned away.

Mallory called after him, "Watch out for that bushwhacker, friend. I don't want to lose that strawberry roan!"

He waved to them and lifted the roan to a lope.

He kept alert on the way through the hills and across 77 range. But the bushwhacker had decided to wait for another day.

He told Lyle Creighton about it that evening, not because the ranch manager could do anything to help but because he wanted to make it clear that in the event of his being murdered the blame should be focused in the right direction.

He'd found Creighton sitting on the ranch house porch smoking his pipe. The story of the attempted killing brought a shocked expression to the man's face.

"You're positive, Ed, that it wasn't one of the rustler crowd?"

"Positive enough to satisfy me."

"And you suspect the rancher who hired Will Vance?"

Raglan frowned, thinking about the man who'd had the deal with Vance, about Frank Amberton, his old friend. He still found it difficult to believe that Amberton would want him murdered. He said, "I don't know, Mr. Creighton. It could have been that rancher, or a man he's hired. Or it could have been Will Vance trying to work off a grudge. Maybe it was somebody sent by Matt Dane. I just don't know."

"What can we do about it?"

"Nothing, until I find out who the bushwhacker is."

"He may make another attempt on your life before you find out," Creighton said. "A successful one."

"That's possible," Raglan said. "And I don't see how to keep him from it."

"There's one precaution you can take. Don't ride anywhere alone.

Raglan made a wry face. "That's something," he said. "My needing somebody to gun-guard me. How'd I ever get to be so important?"

It was a sensible precaution, however, and he took it. Then two days after the attempt on his life, Raglan and some of the 77 hands put a herd on the trail south to Hanlon's Junction on the railroad. It was a small herd, five hundred head, but all prime stock. The cattle were two and three-year-old steers that had been grazed experimentally in fenced pasture since early spring. It had been Raglan's idea to keep them off the open range to fatten them, and Creighton had agreed to the plan on condition that the fencing would not be an expense to 77 Ranch. Raglan had selected a small valley north of ranch headquarters and he and the crew had done the fencing with timber cut in the surrounding hills. The steers had fattened, and the lot was the best beef 77 had yet sent to market.

The drive was being made earlier than Raglan and Creighton had planned because the company officials in Philadelphia had demanded that the ranch show more profit immediately. The decision to ship the steers was Creighton's, but, as he told Raglan, he had no choice. They couldn't wait until beef prices went higher; catering to the whims of the company officials, who kept a steady flow of complaining letters and telegrams coming to 77 Ranch, was Creighton's first consideration.

Raglan took it slow and easy on the drive, in order not to work any weight off the Durham-strain steers, and twelve days passed before he threw the herd into the railroad stocks pens at the Junction and another day before he got them loaded onto the cars. It was Monday when the cattle were loaded, the Monday following the Sunday he had intended to call on Christine. He'd missed out too on dinner at the Ambertons' the previous Sunday. He imagined that Clara Amberton would be put out with him. He supposed Christine would be, too, but in a different way. She would be annoyed because she'd not been able to show him how little she cared that he came calling. He was sure she had made herself absent from the Mallory ranch, as she'd threatened, and gone visiting neighbors farther back in the hills. Christine would be a person to keep her word. Raglan told himself that he'd take her by surprise the coming Sunday.

After seeing the cattle Omaha-bound, he left the crew, cavvy and chuckwagon in charge of Tip Nolan for the return trip to 77 Ranch. He took his saddle and caught the stage to Bennett, boarding it early Tuesday morning. At noon Wednesday, he reached Bennett and obtained a mount at the Star Corral for the remainder of the trip to 77 Ranch.

Creighton called as he rode in, "Ed, I want to see you right away."

The man's curt tone and his turning immediately back into the house told Raglan that something had gone wrong. When he entered the house after putting up his horse, he found Creighton seated at the desk in his comfortable office. The ranch manager was not taking his ease there at the moment, however. He looked harassed.

"Bad news for you, Ed," he said. "I want to say to begin with that I don't like any part of it. I won't say that a mistake has been made, because I believe it's worse than that—a deliberate plot against you." He handed Raglan a paper from the desk. "This telegram arrived yesterday. It was mailed out from the telegraph office at Hanlon's Junction."

The telegram read: *Instruct you demand Raglan's immediate resignation. Letter to follow.* It was signed: *Ainsworth.*

Raglan dropped the telegram onto the desk. "What's the rest of it?"

"A lot has happened in the two weeks you've been away," Creighton told him. "First, the range detective hired by the Tulare Basin Cattlemen's Association showed up at Tomahawk with a steer bearing your RAG brand. It was a fresh burn, still not wholly healed. Matthew Dane had the steer killed and the hide removed. The original brand showed on the inside of the hide, and it was a Tomahawk. Dane and the detective came here with the hide, looking for you. When I told them you were on the trail with a herd, Dane demanded that I fire you when you returned. I said I wouldn't agree to that, I'd have to give you a hearing."

"So he sent a telegram to Crown Land and Cattle Company," Raglan said. "He went over your head."

"He claims he acted for the Association. At any rate, his wire to J. P. Ainsworth did the trick. And since Ainsworth is president of the Crown Land and Cattle Company—well, Ed, if I don't follow his instructions I stand to lose my job. I've got to ask you for your resignation, much as I hate it."

"Don't let it bother you," Raglan said. "It's not the end of the world for me. I'll go back to being a raggedy-pants cowman."

"Stop by before you leave and I'll have your money ready," Creighton said. "I'll give you an extra month's pay, along with what's due you."

"You're convinced I'm being framed?"

"I am. I can't believe that you're a thief."

"Thanks," Raglan said. "That helps a little." He was frowning, but beyond that he showed no emotion. He had to admit to himself that he felt bad about leaving 77 Ranch, but mostly he was just plain sore. He had been whipped without a chance to fight, and that did rankle. He said, "Who is this detective the Association's hired, Lyle?"

"A man named Harnish. Lew Harnish. You know him?"

"No," Raglan said. "But I aim to get to know him."

CHAPTER SEVEN

He left 77 Ranch toward sundown and headed northeast. Two hours later, traveling at a steady lope, he entered the Barrens, a stretch of rough country extending north to his own Squaw Creek graze. He swung due east, and as dusk thickened into nightfall he sighted the lights at Tomahawk a couple of miles off to his right. He was riding the strawberry roan in Sam Mallory's 4M iron, and the gelding showed a lot of bottom, its pace never faltering and its sides hardly blowing. He did rein in to let the horse rest once he got beyond the Barrens, dismounting and having a smoke while he waited.

There was a sickle moon and a myriad of stars, but no night coolness. The day's heat rose from the earth, and the breeze felt hot. It was a night for storms, and far to the northwest lightning flashed. He dragged hard on his cigarette, seeking comfort from it. He'd been lonely enough while living at 77 surrounded by men, but his loneliness almost overwhelmed him now. Lyle Creighton had been decent enough about his "resigning," but he dared not remain friendly toward a man branded rustler.

He'd had no friends among the crew. A man couldn't give orders to a bunch of men as individualistic and independent as cowhands and win their friendship. There was Frank Amberton, of course, but Frank, like Lyle Creighton wouldn't dare show him any friendship now. Still, he was on his way to see Frank— and only partly because of his loneliness and need to see a friendly face. There was something he must find out from Frank Amberton, something more important than whether or not the Ladder A's owner was still his friend. His loneliness was a smaller concern than his danger.

For there was danger still.

Matthew Dane would not be satisfied with merely costing him his job. When Dane struck at a man he did so with all his might and as often as need be to beat his victim down.

Raglan dropped his cigarette, deadened it beneath his boot. The breeze had become a gusty wind, and the lightning was nearer and brighter. He heard the rumble of thunder as he mounted and turned the roan again in the direction of Ladder A.

He covered another half dozen miles through the inky black night before the storm broke about him. He halted with the first spatter of raindrops to remove his slicker from the saddle cantle, and the downpour came by the time he donned it. The lightning and thunder staged a gigantic artillery duel. The wind rose to a gale and the rain fell in torrents. He rode through the storm for another two miles, then saw the gleam of lamplit windows ahead. Riding into the Ladder A ranchyard, he saw that only the ranch house was lighted. The bunkhouse was already dark, the Ladder A hands abed. He rode to the barn, dismounted to open the door, led his horse inside. He left it saddled, closed the door behind him and sprinted across the wide yard to the house.

Frank Amberton had built in the fashion of Matthew Dane, big and solidly. Raglan mounted stone steps to a long roofed porch. He rapped heavily upon the door. The wind-swept rain beat in beneath the roof at him. The door opened, and Clara Amberton peered out at him.

"Ed, for heaven's sakes!" She opened the door wide. "Come in before you drown!"

He entered, dripped water onto the hall floor.

"Clara, I've got to see Frank."

"All right. Take off your hat and slicker."

She pushed the door closed against the force of the storm, and stood by studying him frowningly. She was ready for bed, wearing a wrapper over her nightgown. Her dark hair hung in heavy enamel-black plaits at her shoulders. Her wrapper was a pale green and infinitely becoming. There was a clothestree in the corner beyond the door, and he hooked his hat and slicker on it. She took his arm, led him to the parlor.

It was a huge room extravagantly furnished, and Raglan saw the wet tracks his boots made on the Brussels carpet. Chairs and sofas were plush-covered, and a great center table was laden with bric-a-brac. A grand piano occupied one corner of the room. Despite the night's heat and humidity, a log fire flickered briskly and a book open on a sofa facing the fireplace told him that Clara had been enjoying the warmth of the blaze. It was a gaudy, luxurious room, a perfect setting for what Frank and Clara Amberton had become. They had done well, Raglan found himself thinking; Frank the one-time Texas cowhand and Clara the daughter of a ne'er-do-well townsman whose trade had been carpentering when he was sober enough to work at it.

Clara watched him as he looked around, and finally she said, "You act as though you never saw this room before, Ed. Have you forgotten you visited us before?"

"It seems new and fine all over again."

"I'm glad you like it."

"I wonder if I'll ever have one half as fine."

"You can if you want it badly enough."

"Is that all it takes—mere wanting?" He signed. "Where's Frank? Not in bed?"

"He's in Cheyenne.

"But—"

"On a business trip."

He eyed her with surprise. "If you'd told me, I wouldn't have come barging in like this."

"I couldn't turn you away in this storm, could I? Sit down, Ed. I'll get you a drink. You look as though you could use one."

She left the room. He seated himself, but wasn't comfortable. He feared that his range clothes would soil the chair. Clara returned, bearing two drinks. She laughed when he stared at the one she kept for herself.

"I've learned to drink with my husband," she said. "Whisky makes me feel relaxed, in the most wonderful way. Does that shock you?"

"I'm old fashioned, I guess."

"You like your women to be ladies," she said, mischievously amused. "Frank says he likes me to be a lady in public and something else in private." She held up her glass. "Here's to us, Ed—and to Frank, of course."

He drank with her, thinking: Well, I'll be damned. He'd never known that there was a bit of the hussy in Clara. He had stood up when she re-entered the room, and now she told him to come sit on the sofa with her. She removed her slippers and tucked her bare feet under her as she curled up at one end of it. He sat at the other end and took another swallow of his drink.

"Good whisky. No more barroom rotgut for Frank, eh?"

"New Orleans bourbon. Only the best for Frank."

"The best comes high. He's lucky he can afford to indulge himself."

"It's foolish to be content with shoddy things, Ed."

"I suppose so," he said. "But how does a man get over being foolish?"

"It takes more than hard work," Clara said. "A man has to be clever. What did you want to see Frank about?"

He stared into his glass. The storm raged about the house at the height of its fury, but here in this too-comfortable room was a serene quiet. A thousand storms could batter Ladder A's ranch-house and cause only a weathering of its timbers. Frank's walls were thick and tight, his roof sound. He drank good whisky and had an attractive woman for his bed. But Raglan found himself thinking that for all of that his friend had built on a shaky foundation. Frank and his damn rustling …. Why he should worry about Frank Amberton's dishonesty, he didn't understand. He, not Frank, was the one branded rustler.

He said, "It's not important. It can wait."

She shook her head. "It is important, or you wouldn't have come all the way from Seventy-seven Ranch so late. By the way, we were disappointed when you didn't come to dinner Sunday a week ago."

"I was trailing some beef to the railroad," he said. "Sorry I couldn't make it."

"You're forgiven—since you're here now."

"I should be going."

"Why?"

"That's an odd question."

Clara smiled. "Are you afraid there'll be a scandal if it's known that you called while Frank was away? There won't be. Things have worked out perfectly. I haven't a housekeeper right now, and most of the hands are out on roundup to gather a herd for market. There's only a couple of the men here at headquarters, and no doubt they're asleep. So there's nobody really to know how long you stay. Besides, Frank trusts you—doesn't he, Ed?"

He grinned. "If I had a good looking wife like you, I wouldn't trust any man alone with her." He sobered, seeing that she was not now in a bantering mood. He asked, "Do you really want me to answer that?"

"I know all about Frank's business affairs, Ed."

"You know about my talk with him at the Dane party?"

"Yes."

"And you knew that he had Will Vance—and no doubt some other men—burning his Ladder A brand onto cattle belonging to other ranches?"

"I suspected it," Clara said gravely. "I wasn't sure, and didn't want to be. I never discussed such a thing with Frank—not until he told me you'd caught Vance at it. It's wrong, of course, and foolish. Frank should have known better. But he was desperate. You see, Ed, he went over his head financially when he built Ladder A's headquarters and furnished this house. Besides that, we made that trip East a year ago. We've been reckless with money. Frank's deep in debt to a Cheyenne bank and to an Omaha commission firm with whom he has contracts to supply beef. He turned to mavericking to save himself, but mavericking wasn't quite enough. So he made his foolish deal with Will Vance."

"And how many others?"

"Two or three."

"Has he called them off since I talked to him?"

"Of course he has," Clara said. "You're peeved about it, aren't you, Ed? And worried that somebody else may find out?"

He shrugged. "I don't know about that," he said. "I'm not Frank Amberton's keeper. I've got worries of my own. Or maybe you know about that, since you know all about Frank's business affairs."

She looked at him blankly. "What do you mean?"

He told her about losing his job and the reason for it. He told her too about the attempt on his life that day in the Hatchet Hills. She seemed surprised, horrified. He was almost convinced that she had not known about it.

"I didn't know," she said. "Frank didn't know."

"You're sure he didn't?"

"He'd have told me," Clara said. Then, eyes widening, she said, "You came here thinking that Frank had something to do with all this?"

"He and Matt Dane are as thick as thieves. I figured Dane would have told him."

"I'm not so sure. Matt knows you and Frank used to be good friends. He'd understand that Frank wouldn't have any part of killing you or framing you. That's what it is, isn't it, Ed? You've been framed?"

"That's it," he said. "I did no brand blotting."

"What are you going to do now?"

"I don't know," he said. "Go back to my place on Squaw Creek, I suppose."

Clara took his empty glass, rose to set it and her own on a table. She walked to a window and gazed out into the black, stormy night. There was a green-blue glare of lightning and a great clap of thunder. She started violently, then moved hastily away from the window. She moved aimlessly about the room in her bare feet, and as she passed a bright table lamp her figure was outlined through wrapper and nightgown. She had broad full hips and large breasts and Raglan found himself thinking that she was a lot of woman. She stopped at the piano, let her fingers idle across the keys for a moment of discordant music. Then she returned to the sofa before the fireplace, wriggled her feet into her slippers.

"Why don't you clear off this range, Ed," she said, "and make a fresh start somewhere else?"

"Why?"

"There's nothing but trouble for you here—and I don't want you in trouble."

He rose. "I'd better be on my way," he said.

She looked straight into his eyes. "There's no hurry. I'm not anxious to be alone. Why don't you leave, Ed?"

He smiled. "You're mixing me up."

"Stay here a little longer," she said. "But leave Tulare Basin." She came to him, lay her hands on his shoulders. "Be sensible, darling. For my sake, if not for your own. I've always been fond of you, and it would hurt me if anything bad happened to you."

She slipped her arms about his neck and pressed her body against his. Her lips touched his experimentally, then became moist and clinging. Against his will, he slipped his arms about her and enfolded the warm softness of her against him. It was as though Frank Amberton did not exist, as though they were alone in a stormy world of their own.

Then Clara said, "You will go away, Ed—for me?"

CHAPTER EIGHT

Suddenly Raglan understood what she was doing, and the passion she had aroused in him curdled. He caught her by the shoulders and shoved her from him.

She fell onto the sofa, stunned for a moment. Then she stared at him disbelievingly. Her wrapper and nightgown had been disarranged by his roughness and one shoulder was bared. She had the look of a wanton.

"Ed, what's wrong?"

"You're a little too easy to see through, Clara."

"I don't know what you mean."

"You know, all right," he said. " 'Get a hold on him,' you told yourself, 'and he'll do as you want.' " He shook his head. "Nothing doing, Clara. You may be a big help to Frank in most of his affairs, but this is one time you can't help him."

"Ed, you're so wrong!"

"Wrong, hell. You're scared to death of me. You and Frank. You're afraid I'll let it out that he's a thief. So you want to get me off this range, and you're willing to pay me—in your own sort of coin—to get me to leave it. Well, be scared. I'm staying in Tulare Basin, for keeps."

She started to speak, then pinched her lips together. She saw the hardening of his resolve and realized there was no arguing with him.

He said, "Tell your husband that you tried but—"

She straightened on the sofa but did not bother to cover her exposed shoulder. She said, "What I did doesn't concern Frank personally. He didn't know you were coming here tonight and so he couldn't have asked me to try to influence you. But you're right. I am afraid of you. Frank says that you'd never give him away, but I'm not so sure. You—"

He cut in, "You know now. I've just told you. What I know about Frank Amberton, I'll keep to myself. But if he's still playing with fire, he's apt to be burnt—without my having anything to do with it. Tell him that too."

He swung about and strode from the room.

She cried, "Ed, don't go!" and there was despair in her voice. "Ed—"

He got his hat and slicker in the hall and left the house, plunging through the storm to the barn. He mounted his horse, rode from the barn into the rainy dark. She stood at the doorway of the house, screaming his name as he crossed the ranchyard at a lope. It took him a moment to understand why she wanted him back when she knew that he wouldn't change his mind about staying on the range. Then he realized that she'd been betrayed by her own emotions. She hadn't been able to hold her feelings in check, and now her desire was a genuine and overwhelming thing.

He thought sourly: Let her want me! It seemed no better than she deserved, and now, lonely though he might be, he had no reason to envy Frank Amberton.

Once away from Ladder A, he reined in the roan and tried to decide what his next move would be. He had gone to the Amberton place in the hope of finding some way out of his predicament. It had been a false hope, of course. Frank Amberton would have given him no help if he had been at home.

He wondered whether Clara had lied when she said Frank had not known about the attempt on his life and the maneuver which cost him his job. She was a clever actress, and she may have deceived him on that score. But regardless, Frank Amberton would give Ed Raglan no helping hand. One fact he could hold to, Raglan told himself: Matthew Dane was the man behind the frame-up—and so his next move must be to get at Dane.

And that would be suicide, since the Tomahawk owner had surrounded himself with men who were as much gunmen as cowhands.

There was still a way to get at Dane, however, an around-about way, through Lew Harnish, the Association's range detective. He had no idea of where Harnish might be found, but decided that he probably worked out of Bennett.

He headed for the town, which was half a dozen miles from Ladder A.

He rode through rain the entire way.

The hour was late, the town dark except for a very few lighted windows. He stabled the roan at the Star Corral, then made his way to the business section. Where there were no board side-walks, he strode through gummy mud and ankle-deep puddles. There were two important saloons in Bennett: the Stockmen's Bar, which catered to the men from the big outfits, and McDade's Saloon, which was frequented by the two-bit ranchers and by rid-ers of no visible means of livelihood. The latter was nicknamed the Rustlers' Roost by the big-outfit men, but, oddly enough, it was the quieter of the two. McDade kept an orderly place; he had no percentage girls on the premises and he was big and rough enough to stop any trouble between his customers before it got properly started. Entering McDade's, Raglan found it quieter than usual.

There were only four customers, two at the bar and two at a table, and they evidently required little attention, for Pat McDade, a ruddy-faced man with pomaded hair, was bending over a copy of the Cheyenne *Sun*. By McDade's bored expression, Raglan guessed that he had read the newspaper through before now.

McDade looked up, said, "Hello, Ed," and turned to get bottle and glass. "A good night for ducks, eh?"

Raglan agreed that it was. He removed his dripping hat and slicker, dropped them on a chair and went to the bar. He gestured toward the other customers and said, "Set them up all around, McDade."

One of the pair at the far end of the bar said, "Don't bother, McDade. We're not so thirsty that we have to drink with a big-outfit man."

McDade said, "Mind your manners, Mallory."

Mallory said, "And you mind your own business, McDade."

Raglan studied him with interest, knowing that this would be Christine's brother. Both were her brothers, since the two men there resembled each other. They were lanky, homely men with red hair and reddish bristle on their cheeks. They were as touchy by nature as the girl, but a man could overlook her temper because of her beauty. There was nothing pretty about her brothers, though. They looked boot-tough and wolf-mean.

McDade said ominously, "Jess, hold onto your tongue. Ed Raglan has been a customer of mine since I set up business here in a tent before there ever was a town called Bennett. He's never talked out of turn in my place, and that makes him welcome—big-outfit man or no."

The two Mallorys grinned and winked at each other. Raglan saw that they were spoiling for trouble, and he was in a sour enough mood to welcome whatever they had to offer. But he told himself that he was on the outs with too many people, so he shook his head.

"You've got it wrong, boys," he said. "The latest news is that I'm no longer a big-outfit man. I lost my job at Seventy-seven

Ranch today, and I'll probably be blacklisted among the other big outfits. I'm going back to being a raggedy-pants cattleman." He saw the eagerness fade from the Mallory boys' eyes. He nodded at McDade. "Set them up for everybody, Pat."

The saloonman filled five more shot glasses, one for himself. The Mallorys accepted their drinks a bit sheepishly, and the other two customers came from the table to get theirs. One of the latter two Raglan did not know, but his companion was old J. C. Pierce who ranched at Red Butte. Raglan downed his drink, then motioned for McDade to pour him another. He took out makings and built a smoke.

McDade stood near him, nursing his shot of whisky. Finally he said, "I figured you were fixed for life up there at Seventy-seven, Ed." He pitched his voice low so the others couldn't overhear. "Have a fall-out with Mr. Creighton?"

"No. Creighton and I got along all right," Raglan said, he too keeping his voice down. "Somebody else wanted to be rid of me. You'll be hearing about it soon enough. Listen, Pat—you know a man named Lew Harnish?"

"Yeah. He's been around town for about a month now."

"What doing?"

"You've got me there," McDade said. "When he first showed up, I wondered about him. I pegged him for a professional gambler. He has the looks. But he's not gone to work at the Stockmen's Bar and he didn't approach me about setting up a game here. I see him coming and going, but I don't know what he's up to. Why?"

"He's a detective for the Tulare Basin Cattlemen's Association."

"That's news that will interest a lot of hombres I know."

"Where does he hole up?"

"Over at the hotel, most likely."

"Friends?"

McDade thought about it, then shook his head. "Never saw him with anybody," he said. "Funny thing, Ed, but after you notice him as a stranger a time or two, you quit noticing him. He's just another man around. Does that make sense?"

Raglan nodded. "If he's good at his trade, he'd be good at not being noticed. Well, I'll go over to the hotel and see if he's in."

"Watch your step with him," McDade said. "I've got a sudden hunch that Harnish could turn out to be dangerous."

Raglan paid for the drinks, put on his hat and slicker and left the saloon. The Bennett House stood at an angle across the street from McDade's. It was a two-storied frame building with a false-front which added more height to its façade but failed to make it more imposing than any of the town's other business buildings. A lamp burning on low wick cast a dim glow about the lobby. There was a night bell to fetch the proprietor at such late hours, but Raglan ignored it and reached for the register. He turned back a page to find the name Lew Harnish. The man had registered on July 28. A notation on the same line with the signature and address, which was Cheyenne, revealed that Harnish had been given Room Twelve. Assuming that the man still occupied that room, Raglan examined the keyboard behind the desk. The key to Room 12 hung on the board, which meant that Harnish was not in his room.

He stood there for a moment, thinking that only the Devil himself was likely to know the whereabouts of a range detective, and then he went behind the counter and took the key to Room 12. He went upstairs, let himself into Harnish's room, struck a match and lighted the lamp. He saw the usual grubby cow country hotel room, but if Lew Harnish's quarters were shabby, the man himself was neat.

Harnish had stowed his valise beneath the bed, along with a spare pair of boots. His extra clothing was stacked in the bureau; not a single piece of apparel lay about the room. Harnish was evidently something of a dude, for Raglan counted half a dozen freshly laundered shirts in one drawer and a black string tie for each of them. In the top drawer Raglan found the man's razor, a brush, a comb, a bottle of hair tonic, a jar of pomade, a derringer pistol, and a recent copy of the *National Detective Review*. Obviously, the man was not new to his calling.

There was nothing to tell Raglan whether Harnish was out prowling the range for cattle thieves or loafing around town. He extinguished the lamp, locked the door behind him, went downstairs and returned the key to its place on the board. He left the hotel and headed for the Stockmen's Bar, and despite the late hour and the stormy night there were still a dozen customers.

Five men were playing poker at a table, two were shooting pool, four were bellied up at the bar, while the twelfth man sat at a table with a brassy-haired percentage girl. Raglan knew all but the man with the girl, at least by sight. Hank Mockridge was one of the poker players, as was Jess Owens, foreman for Running W. Tom Drury, owner of the TD outfit, stood at the bar with Amos Mowbrey of the Slash M. The others were cowhands from the big outfits. All except the man who was a stranger to Ed Raglan. He thought: Lew Harnish.

Raglan's arrival caused a ripple of excitement about the wide room, followed by a taut silence. He was the target for every pair of eyes in the place, including the bartender's and the percentage girl's. And from this attention directed his way he realized that everyone here knew what the men at McDade's Saloon hadn't known: that he was through at 77 because Matthew Dane had come up with what seemed damning evidence that he was a rustler.

He'd halted just inside the door to remove his slicker. Two of the poker players were Tomahawk men, and now one, burly Jake

Leach, broke the silence by saying, "In the wrong saloon, ain't you, Raglan?"

"That could be, Jake—if this one is reserved for Tomahawk hands."

"The way I hear, it's reserved for honest men." He shoved back his chair, preparatory to rising. "Want to make something of that, rustler?"

Raglan gave him a flat stare. "Later, Jake. Later I'll be glad to accommodate you. Right now I've got something more important on my mind."

Turning his back on the Tomahawk rider, he walked toward the man he believed to be Lew Harnish. He was quite a dude with slicked down hair and a dapper mustache. He wore a dark gray suit, white shirt and black string tie. McDade had been right; this Harnish had the appearance of a professional gambler. But his hat, there on the table, was the broad-brimmed headgear usually worn on the range, and his boots marked him as a riding man. He was in his late thirties, Raglan judged, swarthy of complexion, of medium height, on the lean side. His eyes were that pale gray that suggested chilled steel. They went wary now, watching Raglan.

Raglan said, "Lew Harnish?"

"That's right. But you have the advantage of me, sir."

"My name was mentioned a couple of seconds ago."

"I'm afraid I wasn't paying attention."

"All right. I'll introduce myself. Ed Raglan."

Harnish took a cigar from his vest pocket, bit off the tip and struck a match. "I see," he said, and puffed the cigar alight. "What can I do for you, Raglan?"

"Answer a few questions."

Harnish nodded, then glanced at the woman. "Josie, beat it."

The woman took on a sulky pout but rose and moved away.

Raglan draped his slicker over the back of the chair she vacated, and lay his hands atop it. He was sharply aware that every other man in the place was watching and listening, and that Jake Leach probably was trying to decide whether or not to force the quarrel he'd failed to get started. He ignored them and kept his gaze steadily on Harnish.

"Where'd you get that hide, friend?"

"Out on the range. Where else?"

"You just happened on the cow and saw a fresh RAG burned on it."

"It was pointed out to me."

"Ah," Raglan said. "Now we're getting somewhere. Who pointed it out?"

Harnish considered a moment, puffing on his cigar. "I'm not at liberty to say," he said. "I reported the matter to the Tulare Basin Cattlemen's Association. You'll have to go to the Association for the information you want."

Raglan smiled, but it was merely a baring of his teeth. "Harnish, I've been framed and you helped do the framing. I can be tough as all hell. Now, who pointed out that cow to you? Talk up, man. Don't make me beat it out of you."

"Be sensible, Raglan. Don't lose your head."

"Worry about yourself, friend. Name the man."

"I told you—"

"Let's go for a walk, Harnish."

"In the rain?" Harnish said. "No, thanks. I don't want to get my suit spotted."

Raglan lifted his slicker from the chair. "I said we're going for a walk. Either you walk out of here with me, or I'll drag you."

Harnish still puffed on his cigar, but it had gone out. He reached into his vest pocket as though searching for a match. Raglan saw a glint of metal, and remembered the derringer pistol he'd seen in the man's room. Harnish was sneaking a twin to it from his pocket. Raglan flung the slicker into the man's face, then hipped the table aside and grabbed the wicked little weapon from his hand.

Harnish threw the slicker away and leaped from his chair, but Raglan collared him before he could escape. For a moment Raglan was sure that he would have his way with the man, but then Jake Leach and the other Tomahawk hand, Lefty Greer, came at him. He swung Harnish around as a shield, but the other two were too quick for him. Leach struck him a clubbing blow to the back of the neck, and there was enough power behind it to buckle his knees.

CHAPTER NINE

Leach kneed him in the face as he went down, and Greer booted him as he lay helpless on the floor. He lost the derringer and was too dazed to make use of his own gun. He sprawled there, face down and full of splintering pain. Then he pressed his hands against the floor, levering himself to his knees. They permitted him to gain his feet, then closed in again.

He saw them but fuzzily, and struck clumsy blows. One wild punch did catch Lefty Greer solidly in the face, causing him to yelp with hurt. The next instant he was clouted heavily by Leach, stunned to the point of paralysis, and they battered him at will until he collapsed. Even then he struggled to rise. He would have made it but Greer said, "Damn, but he's a tough bastard!" and booted him again, this time to the side of the head.

He was barely conscious now, and they dragged him from the saloon and dumped him into the mud of the street. Two riders coming along through the rainy dark at a lope pulled up short to keep from trampling him.

He heard Jake Leach say to the riders, "He s your kind. Maybe you want to look after him."

One of the riders dismounted, helped him to his feet, held him erect. He recognized the Mallory brothers, and it was Jess helping him. After a moment Jess let him stand alone, but caught hold of him again when his knees gave way.

"Bucko," Jess said, "you're sure in a bad way."

There was some discussion between the two, and it ended with the decision to take him to McDade's Saloon. He was out on his feet the entire distance, and would not have made it without help. McDade was closing his place for the night.

The other Mallory, Steve, said, "This man's in bad shape, Pat. Somebody's got to take him in."

McDade peered at them from his door. "Who is it?"

"That Raglan hombre."

"Oh. All right, bring him in."

Jess Mallory half carried, half dragged him inside and eased him onto a chair. "We found him outside the Stockmen's Bar," he told McDade. "A couple Tomahawk riders gave him the bum's rush."

"I've seen better looking dead men."

"Yeah. He's a mess, all right. You'll take care of him?"

"Sure," McDade said. "Close the door on your way out."

Raglan leaned forward, lowering his head into his hands. It throbbed with pain. He was dripping blood onto the floor. McDade brought him a stiff drink of whisky, holding the glass when his hands proved too shaky. The saloonman fetched a basin of water and a cloth, washed his face clean of blood and mud. There was a deep gash at his left temple. McDade said, "Ed, this will sting," and swabbed the cut with raw whisky. After a few minutes the bleeding stopped, and the pain was eased by the big dose of whisky taken inwardly.

McDade said, "What's going on, Ed?"

"I got a little rough with Lew Harnish. Jack Leach and Lefty Greer got a lot rougher with me."

"What's it all about?"

"Harnish has a hide with the Tomahawk brand blotched over by my old RAG brand."

"Frame-up?"

"What else?"

"Who's behind it?"

Raglan's battered face turned ugly. "That's what I've got to find out. And when I find out, there's going to be hell to pay. I've been shot at, framed, beaten up—and, by damn, I'm not taking any more such guff." He forced himself to his feet. "Thanks for doctoring me up, Pat. I'll be on my way, so you can turn in."

"Spend the night here," McDade said. "I'll loan you a blanket and you can bed down in a back room. You're in no condition to go anywhere."

Raglan's legs were wobbly, and he had to grab the chair to stay on his feet. "I'll have to take you up on that," he said. "Thanks again."

His face, in the morning, was a mass of bruises. He had a black eye, a cut over his right cheekbone as well as the one at his left temple, and a badly swollen jaw. His head still ached, and he had sore spots everywhere. Looking at himself in the mirror on the wall of McDade's living quarters, he saw, along with the marks left by the fists of the Tomahawk men, the smoldering anger in his own eyes, and was startled by its intensity. He knew then that he was a man possessed, that he would have no peace of mind until he evened the score with whoever had planned his downfall. He'd seen that chill, calculating resolution in the eyes of other men, a time or two, men who had been pushed too far. It wasn't a pretty thing, but awesome.

McDade had risen an hour ahead of him, and had taken his levis and ducking jacket outside to brush the dried mud off them. His clothes looked fairly respectable again, if he did not. McDade also had prepared breakfast, and after they'd eaten he asked, "What now, Ed?"

"Harnish again."

"I have a notion he'll be a hard man to find."

"I'll find him."

"To try to make him admit he helped frame you?"

"At least to tell me who pointed out that cow with the blotched brand."

"If it was a Tomahawk cow," McDade said, "you'll come up against Matt Dane. As a friend, I advise you to let well enough alone."

"Thanks. But that's not advice I can take."

"Well, if it's Dane who framed you and you try to prove it, I wouldn't want to be in your boots for all the cattle in Tulare Basin." The saloonman grunted worriedly. "But luck to you, Ed."

"Thanks, Pat. Thanks for everything."

The morning was crystal clear. The sun, already high, was baking the mud of Bennett's main street hard and dry. Raglan went first to the Stockmen's Bar to recover his hat and slicker which he'd lost during the fight with the Tomahawk men. The door stood open to the sun, and a swamper, a seedy old man, was sweeping the floor in a halfhearted fashion. The hat and slicker lay upon a table. Raglan reshaped and donned the hat, slung the slicker over his shoulder and headed for the Bennett House. He found the hotel owner, Jim Hake, in the lobby.

"Harnish," he said. "Is he still in his room?"

"No. He went out early. What happened to your face, Raglan?"

"I had an accident. Any idea where he went?"

"No. But it was out of town, I imagine."

"How come you imagine that?"

"He was wearing spurs. He wouldn't wear them unless he expected to ride."

"Keeps his horse at the Star Corral, does he?"

"Yeah," Hake said, and couldn't help asking, "Trouble between you two?"

Raglan nodded and went out, going to the livery stable at the end of the main street. Cleve Arnold operated the Star Corral. He also dealt in horses and mules. He was a lanky, shrewd-eyed, tobacco-chewing trader. Raglan found him in his cubbyhole office.

"Did Lew Harnish take his horse out this morning?"

"Yeah. About two hours ago."

"You notice which way he headed?"

"Toward Tomahawk," Arnold said, "with a couple of that outfit's hands." He spat tobacco juice at a brass cuspidor beside his rolltop desk, giving Raglan a sly look. "Heard some talk this morning that you had a set-to with him and the other two. Any truth to it?"

Raglan figured that his battered face was answer enough. He felt anger roiling in him because he'd slept late and let Harnish get away. Then he realized that if he had risen early, he wouldn't have been able to get at the detective. Leach and Greer had stayed overnight in Bennett to protect Harnish, and now were escorting him to Tomahawk where he would be beyond Raglan's reach. But two could play a waiting game, and Raglan had a hunch that Harnish's patience would run out before his own—for while he waited, he would keep busy re-establishing himself at Squaw Creek.

He reached the Squaw early next morning, riding the Mallory roan and leading under pack a stocky gray gelding he'd bought from Cleve Arnold. Later, after he'd returned the roan to Sam Mallory, the gray would serve as his mount.

This was rough country, and a range of craggy bluffs separated it from the rolling prairie land that made up the main portion of Tulare Basin. The Squaw was a wanton little stream, fast-flowing in a narrow channel toward a high-walled gorge of

the same name. Within the gorge, which was a half dozen awesome miles long, the swift water did not sing a mere siren's song
but gave off a tumultuous, agonized wailing which, where the
course of it was most torturous, often rose to a screaming roar.
Raglan knew of the Squaw's ordeal, for he had ventured through
the narrow, twisting canyon on several occasions. It had been
something of a feat each time, and he doubted that any other
rider had ever been foolhardy enough to make the trip.

There were other, less treacherous canyons, and numerous
small valleys. There were rock fields, sand flats, eroded buttes.
Grass was where a cow found it, and never abundant, but Raglan
had always believed that this country—his range, since he alone
had ever ranched here—would permit the running of at least
five thousand head of cattle. If a man had that many cattle. He'd
never been that big a cowman.

Riding through a gap in the range of bluffs toward his buildings, he had an occasional glimpse of cattle in the brush. The
critters were wilder than on the main Basin range, and fled at
the sight or scent of him. That was due to the absence of riders
here. It was possible that, despite the scramble after mavericks,
no riders had worked this back country and thus he would be the
owner of a considerable little herd. The calf crop of even a couple
hundred head for two years was no small thing, and he would be
wise to burn his RAG iron onto the unbranded stock as soon as
possible.

His buildings were located between the creek and a pine-
timbered slope, no more than half a mile from the entrance to
Squaw Gorge. Seeing them now, for the first time in two years,
he became the victim of confused emotions. The one-room cabin
and the small log barn were in a state of disrepair that depressed
him, but at the same time he experienced the pride of owner-
ship that came to a man at times despite the meagerness of his

property. His pride curdled when he remembered that he had done his homesteading in a section where no other men cared to settle, but then he found a satisfaction in the knowledge that he had put up his buildings with his own two hands—and could make them livable again by his own efforts. A sense of loneliness stole over him as he drew near the place, but then he reminded himself that he also had been lonely at 77 Ranch.

And so he faced reality. This was his homecoming, and this time he would put down his roots. There would be no second offer of a ranch foreman's job to bait him away. He would have to quit thinking of the place as a cow camp, and regard it as his ranch headquarters. And no matter whether his spirits were high or low, whether he was lonely or not, he had to live with his feelings and master them.

Grass and brush grew in the yard between house and barn. The roofs of both buildings needed repairs; that of the barn sagged perilously. The door of the cabin hung by one leather hinge, and when he swung it open, the hinge parted. He stood the plank door against the outer wall, then went inside. A squirrel scampered past him in sudden flight. The stone fireplace was at the north wall, his bunk at the south. In the center of the room was a plank table with a bench at either side. Except for a cupboard in which to store food and cooking utensils there was nothing else. It was a crude shelter, not a real home. Dust filmed everything, and there was the dank odor of a building long closed to sun and air.

He returned to his horses, removed the roan's saddle and the gray's pack. The corral fence was broken down in several places, so he staked out the animals. He carried provisions and gear inside, then started a fire to rid the cabin of dampness. He cooked a meal of bacon, biscuits and coffee, and after eating he went to the barn seeking a couple bundles of shake shingles that had been left from when he put up the buildings. He spent the afternoon repairing the cabin roof and hanging the door on new hinges made of pieces cut from a spare belt. He told himself that he would buy hardware hinges, the next time he went to town. It was sundown by the time he had the door back in place, and he knocked off to rustle up his supper.

He went to bed at nightfall, to ward off loneliness.

And in the morning he rode out across the range, sighting more cattle than he had expected. He knew now that no maverickers had worked the Squaw Creek country. He knew too that there were more mavericks here than could be credited to his own small herd, and understood why. Cattle from the main portion of Tulare Basin had drifted into the rough country. Cattle in the 77 iron, in the Tomahawk, in others. These cattle had dropped calves, and they had gone unbranded. Mavericks .... Raglan debated it with himself, and made his decision. He was looking out for Ed Raglan from now on, and eventually these mavericks were going into his RAG brand.

After his noon meal, he set out again. He rode the gray and led the roan by a halter rope. He headed west along the creek, following it downstream to the entrance to the canyon. The Squaw tumbled into the gorge over a series of waterfalls. A thunderous roar rose from the depths, and the air was filled with sunlit spray that had the colors of a rainbow. At first glance there appeared to be no footing for horses, and Raglan's animals became skittish because of the roar of cascading water and tried to shy away from the canyon's rim. He dismounted and tied the roan's rope to the horn of the gray's saddle, then led the gray by its reins. They followed him reluctantly, wall-eyed with fright as they descended the treacherous, rocky slope by a series of difficult switchbacks. Even when he reached the canyon floor, the going was only slightly less difficult due to the narrowness of the gorge and the huge rocks littering it.

After perhaps half a mile, however, the gorge widened somewhat and there were fewer rocks. Gradually it spread until fifty yards separated the towering walls, and Raglan got back into the gray's saddle. Midway, the south wall bowed, and between it and the creek was a bench of about an acre in size. It was the only pleasant spot in the entire forbidding gorge, among the grass and brush and scrub trees, and here, wide and shallow, the Squaw lowered its voice to a murmur.

Raglan halted to rest his horses. He built a smoke, relaxing. This spot was a glaring contrast to the awesome bleakness of the rest of the gorge, with its soft green grass and foliage and the pattern of sunlight and shadows. It occurred to him that here a man came as far from the outer world as he could get, and when in a troubled frame of mind, it was a good place for him to be. It might be man's nature to fight back against his enemies, but in every human there was an urge to run and hide. Raglan's mood mellowed. He had found a sort of peace here, even when he knew that he could linger but a few minutes.

He rode on when his cigarette burned short, and beyond the bench the going became rough again. The western end of it was as difficult to traverse as the eastern end, and Raglan, though aware that by traveling this way he saved himself a dozen miles on the way to the Mallory ranch, wondered just why he ventured through the gorge. The answer seemed to be that he found it a challenge, that he derived a sort of satisfaction in going where other riders feared to travel.

It had taken him most of the afternoon to work his way through the canyon's half dozen torturous miles, and come from it into a range of low rock hills. Once through the rock hills he had timbered heights before him, and comparatively easy going the last few miles to the Mallory ranch. He descended a slope just north of the buildings, quartering down it, and saw Christine watching him from the back door of the house. As he reined in, she asked, "For heaven's sakes, Raglan, where did you come from?"

"From my place on Squaw Creek."

"Yes, but—"

He knew why she was puzzled. She knew he had ridden in from the direction of Squaw Gorge, but couldn't believe he had come through the gorge. He told her he had done just that.

Puzzlement turned to wonder. "You can get through the gorge? Why, I always heard that nobody could ride through there"

He said, "I can," and dismounted. "I've come to return the roan. Your father isn't around?"

"No. Just turn the bronc out onto the range."

He relieved the roan of the halter and sent it away with a slap to the rump. He turned back to Christine to find her gazing at him in an almost friendly way. He understood why she felt more tolerant now. She'd heard from her brothers that he no longer was a big-outfit man, and so she could be civil.

"Jess and Steve told me you got beat up," she said. "By the looks of your face, they sure told the truth."

"You should have seen me the morning after the fight," he said. "I'm obliged to your brothers for giving me a helping hand that night. Tell them I said 'thanks.' "

She nodded. "I'll tell them. So you lost your job as well as got a beating, did you?"

"That's right."

"Why?"

"I stepped on somebody's toes."

Christine seated herself on the doorstep. "Tell me about it."

He hunkered down, took out makings, and told her about it while rolling a cigarette. He intended at the start to tell only of how he'd been asked to resign as 77 Ranch foreman by Lyle Creighton, and about his seeking out Lew Harnish. But he went on from there, telling her the whole story from the day he had caught Will Vance altering the brand on a 77 cow. He spoke of the Vigilante meeting at Tomahawk Ranch the night of the party, of his visit to Ladder A to see Frank Amberton, and of his failure to find Amberton at home. He held back only two things: Clara Amberton's behavior, and the fact that Will Vance had been in Amberton's hire. He didn't want to tarnish the woman's reputation or throw suspicion on his old friend.

Christine listened intently, and fell into a study when he finished. She sat leaning forward, her arms about her knees. A wave of her coppery hair had tumbled down over her forehead. He could lift his hand and touch her hair, and he was tempted to do it. He dragged hard on his cigarette, trying to hold back an upsurge of feeling. Christine in her faded calico was somehow more seductive than Clara Amberton had been in nightgown and wrapper, and without trying to be.

She said, "So now you're back on your Squaw Creek range, just another raggedy-pants cowman?

"But not for long."

"Oh? You'll be going back to some big outfit?"

"Not that," he said. "I'm going to grow. I'm going to build my outfit into a big one. I've seen how the owners of the big outfits live, and it's a good way to live. There's nothing in grubbing for a skimpy living. Maybe it'll take me ten years or twenty, but no matter how long, I'm going to make something of my Squaw Creek ranch."

Christine was skeptical. "I've heard Sam Mallory talk like that. And he's still grubbing for a skimpy living."

"Maybe his luck was bad."

"And yours isn't?"

"I'm going to make my own luck from now on."

"That's a hardscrabble range you're on," Christine said. "I've heard Pa and the boys say so. They claim that nobody with the sense of a jugheaded mule would run cattle over there."

"I'll prove them wrong."

"That I want to see."

"You'll see," he said. "Just give me a little time."

She studied him for a moment, then said, "You're pretty sure of yourself, aren't you? You got something up your sleeve, Raglan?"

He was thinking of the mavericks in the Squaw Creek country, but decided not to speak of them to the girl. If he told her about them and she mentioned it to her menfolks, they would almost certainly come onto the range with their 4M branding-iron. He wasn't sharing those unbranded cattle with anyone, if he could help it.

He laughed and said, "Maybe I do have something up my sleeve."

Christine rose. "Well, I wish you luck. But ten or twenty years is a mighty long time."

He said, "I guess it is, at that. I'll try to make it a shorter wait."

She said nothing to that.

He dropped his cigarette, flattened it under his boot-heel. He went to his horse and swung to the saddle. He lifted his hat to her.

Christine said, "Stop by again, Raglan."

She turned into the house too quickly to see the smile that came to his bruised face. It was the smile of a man suddenly sure of himself—and of the woman he had marked for his own.

He rode out feeling buoyant of spirit. He could bear the loneliness of the Squaw Creek country, now that Christine Mallory wasn't beyond his reach. She'd let him know that by inviting him to come again—to call on her, actually. But he felt a bit sheepish too about having talked so much. He'd bragged like a schoolboy showing off for a girl who'd caught his fancy. But he was in such a good humor that he could laugh at himself. He lifted the gray to a lope.

He took the long way back to Squaw Creek, for the day was nearly gone and he was not so foolhardy that he would venture into the gorge at night.

CHAPTER TEN

H e spent the following day repairing the corral fence, felling scrub trees on the nearby slope for posts and poles. He gave the barn roof his attention next, and three days passed before it was repaired to his satisfaction. He worked with a right good will, a man with ambition and, because of an auburn-haired girl, high hopes. He kept telling himself while working that in a year or two, as money came in from cattle sales, he would put up larger, more substantial buildings—the sort that would last a lifetime, the sort to which a man could bring a wife.

The repairs completed, he got his RAG branding iron from the barn, cleaned it of rust, and went mavericking. Unbranded cattle were not difficult to find, but the work was almost too much for one man. He had to rope the wild critters, drag them to his branding fire, bulldog them, hogtie them, apply the hot iron. He had to gather brush for the fire, as well, and more than once it burned down to a handful of embers while he was chasing a cow. But the first day he burned his brand on thirteen mavericks, and on twenty-one the second. At the end of a week his herd had increased by more than a hundred head. As he'd expected, he spotted numerous cattle in outside brands. These he did not touch.

As the mavericks grew scarce on the range close to his ranch headquarters, he worked farther out each day. In time he would have to set up a camp at a distance from his buildings, and work the isolated portions of the range from that base. He was still returning to his headquarters each night the second week, however, and rode in one sundown to find Bart Somers there.

Somers had made himself at home. He'd off-saddled his horse and put it up in the corral. He was lounging in the cabin doorway, a tin cup in his hand.

"Made a pot of coffee, Ed," he said. "Hope you don't mind."

"No. But you could have had supper ready for me."

"Didn't know when you'd get in. Want me to rustle it up now?"

"I guess I can stand one meal of your cooking."

Somers's devil-may-care grin flashed. "My cooking never hurt me, bucko."

He went inside, while Raglan put up his horse and washed up at the creek. Somers had a meal of bacon, beans and biscuits on the fire when Raglan entered the cabin.

He said, "Doing some mavericking, Ed?"

"A little. Burning my brand on a few slicks."

"A few?" Somers laughed. "Don't hand me that. I know this range is overrun with mavericks. I've been through here more than once during the past few months. A time or two I told myself I'd come in and set up camp and do some mavericking on my own. Never got around to it"

"Greener pastures elsewhere, eh?"

"That's about it. No use working the back-country when it's easier to handle a long rope and a running iron closer to civilization—and to the shipping point."

"Been busy at it lately?"

"Nope. I've been taking a vacation."

"Hiding out?"

"Sort of," Somers said. "I got your message. I stopped by to say 'thanks.' "

Raglan said, "Forget it."

They did not talk more until after they'd eaten. Then Somers said, "You delivered that message for a lady?"

"Well, yes."

"Laurie Dane?"

"That's right."

Somers's coarsely handsome face lighted up. "Figured so," he said. "There's a girl, that Laurie. A kind of girl to make a man glad he is a man."

"She can be trouble, Bart."

"But a nice kind of trouble. I'm on my way to see her."

Raglan stared, frowning. "You're what?"

Somers laughed. "Why not?" he said. "Laurie and I are real good friends. Her sending me that warning proves that she can't forget Bartie-boy."

"You go to Tomahawk you'll stick your neck in a noose or get your head blown off, Bartie-boy. Your name hasn't been taken off the Vigilante list."

"Tomorrow's Saturday. By late afternoon most all the Tomahawk hands will be on their way to town. All I have to do is to let Laurie know I'm around and she'll meet me at Tomahawk's old horse camp at Drum Lake."

"Listen, Bart, you'd better take my advice and—"

"Can't do it. I'm itching to see that Laurie girl."

Raglan started to say more, but saw that no argument would convince the man that a visit to Tomahawk would be folly. In a way, Bart Somers was a kid who'd never grown up. He enjoyed getting himself into scrapes. Sooner or later he would trip and fall and hurt himself.

Somers said, grinning, "I'll get to Tomahawk headquarters about midnight. Laurie and I had a system when I worked there. We left a sign at a certain place when one or the other wanted to go to the horse camp. I'll Injun up to Tomahawk headquarters, leave the sign for her to see in the morning, and then head for the camp. Nobody'll be the wiser."

Raglan said, "You poor fool."

Somers chuckled, rose from the table and picked up his hat. "I'll stop by on my way back to my hideout, he said, "and show you what a poor fool I am."

"Bart, it's not worth the risk."

"Laurie? Don't be loco, bucko."

"Well, it's your funeral," Raglan said.

He walked outside with Somers and watched him rope and saddle his horse.

Mounted, Somers said, "By the way, I heard you were trying to get hold, of a hombre named Lew Harnish. If you're still interested in him, maybe you'd like to know he's quit hiding out at Tomahawk. He's back at Bennett."

"How do you know that?"

"A little bird told me."

"A little bird came to your hideout, eh?"

"I've got friends in Bennett," Somers said. "They keep me posted. That's how I heard about you losing your job and coming back here to the Squaw. Harnish is a range detective for the Association?"

"That's right."

"Going after him?"

"Yeah. If you're sure he's left Tomahawk."

"My friends never give me bum steers," Somers said. "Need any help with him?"

"No, thanks."

"Well, I'll be seeing you," Somers said. "Me, I'd rather be hunting my kind of game than yours. That Harnish can't be half as pretty as Laurie Dane."

He rode off, laughing.

Raglan stood there looking after him, in a troubled frame of mind. He couldn't shake off the feeling that Somers would get something other than what he hoped for once he reached Tomahawk range.

He took a bath in the chill waters of Squaw Creek in the morning, lathering himself heavily with yellow soap. He shaved. He slicked down his hair. He put on his spare clothes, then saddled the gray and set out for Bennett.

He took it slow and easy, since the gelding had been worked hard ever since he started mavericking, and night fell before he reached town. He put the gray up at the Star Corral, then had supper at the Welcome Cafe. After his meal he went to McDade's Saloon. It being Saturday night, all Bennett's business places were open and busy. McDade's was fairly crowded, his patrons as usual mostly two-bit cattlemen. Sam Mallory and his two sons sat at a table with old J. C. Pierce, one of their neighbors. Raglan stopped at the bar, got a bottle and a glass from McDade, then went to the Mallorys' table. Because of the whisky he brought with him, he was welcomed with enthusiasm. The Mallorys and Pierce had empty glasses in front of them. After filling his own glass, Raglan set the bottle in the center of the table.

"Drink up, gents."

The welcome had come from the Mallorys, and now. as Sam reached for the bottle, Pierce said, "What's that old saying? Beware Greeks bearing gifts—"

Sam said, "Raglan's no Greek, J. C. He's a Texan."

Raglan laughed. "J. C. means beware of big-outfit men. I'm not a big-outfit man nowadays, J. C. Haven't you heard?"

"Nope. It's news to me."

"I'm ranching on my own again, over at Squaw Creek."

"And I'm at Red Butte. That makes us neighbors."

"Yeah," said Raglan. "We're only about forty miles apart. Country's getting crowded."

He pushed Pierce's glass across the table so Sam Mallory could fill it. He felt a little sorry for the old man. Pierce had reached three score and ten, and the passing years had marked him. His leathery skin was eroded by time and hardship; he had a shriveled look. His eyes were still bright in his seamed, dark face, perhaps with that spark of hope to which all raggedy-pants cowmen held to the very end. J. C. Pierce hadn't many years left, and by rights, it seemed to Raglan, he should now know the ease of retirement instead of trying to eke out a livelihood in the cattle business. He wondered how a man so old did keep going as a two-bit rancher. Operating a one-man spread was hard work for a man in his prime, as Raglan had learned these past two weeks at Squaw Creek. He found himself thinking, That's not for me. He was increasingly determined to lift himself above the poverty of the back country cattlemen. He was resolved not to end up a J. C. Pierce, old and alone and hardly able to keep body and soul together. He placed the filled glass before the old man.

Sam Mallory had poured for his sons too, and now he filled his own glass. "Glad you happened along, Ed. The lot of us are find of short of drinking money tonight." He lifted his glass. "*Salud,* as we used to say down on the Rio Bravo."

"*Salud.*"

They all drank, Pierce afterwards licking his lips and looking yearningly at the bottle. Raglan pushed it across the table and told Pierce to help himself.

Sam Mallory said, "I'm kind of surprised to see you in town, Ed."

"How so?"

"Well, you've already had trouble with Tomahawk. I figured you wouldn't give them a chance to jump you again. They're likely to, now you've been tagged as a rustler."

"They'll be leery of me," Raglan said. "They know I won't be so easy to jump a second time—that they'll have to buck my gun."

Jess Mallory said, "You see Bart Somers yesterday, Raglan?"

He nodded. "Bart stopped at my place and ate supper with me. Why?"

Jess shrugged. "I'm just wondering what became of him. He passed our place in the morning and said he'd be back after he saw you. But he didn't show up."

Raglan said, "He changed his mind after leaving your place, then. He had some fool idea of going to Tomahawk."

They all stared at him. Jess finally said, "Fool idea is right. Why would he go to Tomahawk when he knows it's a Vigilante outfit—and his name's on the Vigilante list?" He didn't wait for a reply. "I get it. He wanted, to get to see Matt Dane's daughter. That right, Raglan?"

"So he told me."

"The crazy galoot."

"I advised him against it, but—well, he wouldn't take advice."

"Was he going right to Tomahawk headquarters?"

Raglan nodded. "He planned to ride in there at midnight. He and the Dane girl had arranged some kind of a signal, back when he worked at Tomahawk, to tell each other when they were to get together. Bart figured on fixing the signal for her to see in the morning, then going on to Drum Lake to wait for her." He shook his head. "He's running a mighty big risk, the way I see it. But maybe he's sure he can see the girl without being spotted by any Tomahawk riders."

"Anyway, it's his neck he's risking," Jess said. "And it's none of our business, I guess, if he wants to stick it into a noose."

They discussed Somers for a while, all in agreement that he was a likable but ornery cuss and, because of his wild streak, certainly headed for real trouble. Raglan had another drink with them, then rose and, leaving them to kill the bottle, left McDade's.

He paused outside the saloon, watching the activity along the street. Like all cow towns, Bennett took on a sort of gala holiday air on Saturdays with folks coming in from all over the Basin. There were also numerous dirt farmers and their families, homesteaders, from Aspen Meadows outside the Basin. The farmers' heavy wagons stood along both sides of the street. Their women and children were in and out of the stores, and the farmers themselves gathered in small groups to talk of the weather and of crops. Few of the Aspen Meadows men visited the saloons. Like all homesteaders, they were always short of cash and could spare little for drinking and gambling. There were ranch rigs too: buckboards, light spring wagons, a buggy or two. Every hitchrack was lined with saddle horses. The doorways of the business places stood wide open, casting patches of yellow lamplight into the street and onto the faces of the people.

Raglan turned in the direction of the Stockmen's Bar, meeting Len Hibner in front of the Welcome Cafe. Hibner repped for the law in Tulare Basin. He had been sent out from the sheriff's office at the county seat, and he had an office of his own and a one-room lock-up in a squat log building here in Bennett. He collected taxes and tried to keep a semblance of law and order, but he was an inadequate little man. He came only to Raglan's shoulder, partly because of a lack of stature and partly because of a pronounced stoop. A law badge usually made a man aggressive, but Hibner's manner was always slightly apologetic. He looked a little startled when Raglan spoke his name.

"Something I can do for you?"

"You seen Lew Harnish around town tonight, Len?"

"Yeah. I saw him about an hour ago."

"Where?"

"Going into the Stockmen's Bar." Hibner was uneasy. "Look, Raglan; I heard about you and Harnish having trouble some time ago. You're not aiming to start it up again, are you?"

"I just want a few words with him," Raglan said. "Not trouble."

He crossed the street, passing Tip Nolan and another 77 cowhand, and entered the saloon. It was crowded and noisy, and he halted just inside the doorway to look for Harnish. The range detective was not at the bar, nor at any of the tables, nor among the men shooting pool at the rear of the room. Several men well known to Raglan glanced his way, but none acknowledged his nod. Evidently the story of the hide with his forged RAG brand blotching the Tomahawk brand was known by all the big-outfit people. He thought, To hell with them, and turned to leave.

He was halted by a voice bellowing, "You there, Raglan!"

He saw burly Jake Leach shove away from mid-bar and come toward him on the rubbery legs of a drunk. The Tomahawk man's shout had reached to every corner of the place, and now there was an abrupt diminishing of noise and activity. Aware that he had attracted the crowd's attention, Leach grinned and swelled with importance. He halted directly before Raglan, thumbs hooked in his gunbelt. He was just drunk enough to be nasty, Raglan realized. Drunk enough to push this along until something happened.

Raglan said, "Get it said, Jake."

"I told you once before this place is reserved for honest men."

"I remember the occasion."

"But you never learn, do you, rustler?"

"I've learned one thing lately, Jake."

Leach thought he was doing a fine job of baiting. He glanced around at the rapt gathering, grinning hugely. "What's that you learned, rustler?"

"That somebody—maybe your boss—can use a running iron to frame a man."

"Meaning Matthew Dane?"

"Who else, Jake? You work for Tomahawk, don't you?"

From over at the bar Lefty Greer called, "Jake, you letting him get away with talk like that about Matt Dane?"

That put it directly up to Leach. He hesitated, indecision clouding his tough face. Then he yelled, "Damn if I'll take that kind of talk from a cow thief!"

He lunged at Raglan, striking a clumsy blow.

Raglan had made up his mind not to be caught off guard as he had been on his last visit to the Stockmen's Bar. He blocked Leach's punch and drove his fist to the Tomahawk man's chin. Leach's head rocked far back, and for a moment he hung off balance and defenseless. Raglan caught him next in the midriff, doubling him up. A third blow, this to the base of the skull, finished it. Jake Leach dropped heavily at Raglan's feet, face down, and did not try to rise. Even as Leach went down, Raglan grabbed for his gun and brought it to bear on Lefty Greer. He surprised the second Tomahawk man with his gun half drawn, and he said, "Be smart, Lefty."

Greer froze, his weapon still not clear of its holster. There was a wildness in his eyes for a few seconds, and then he let his gun slide back into its holster.

Raglan said, "Keep on being smart, Lefty," and backed out of the saloon.

He had an instinctive foreknowledge that the man wouldn't heed the warning, and so he went quickly to the corner of the building. He faced about at the mouth of the dark alleyway between the saloon and the neighboring building, and at that instant Greer came running to the street with his gun in his hand.

Tip Nolan and the other 77 cowpuncher were still standing before the saloon, and Greer, his voice shrill with excitement, yelled, "Raglan! Where'd he get to?"

Nolan gestured toward the alleyway, and began a hasty retreat.

Greer whirled, swung his gun up to bead Raglan. Still hoping to avoid gunplay, Raglan called, "Don't be a damn fool, Lefty!" The blast of the gun came as he spoke, and he heard the slug strike the plank wall beside mm. He hesitated no longer, but fired as Greer readied another shot. An incoherent cry ripped from the throat of Greer. He dropped his gun, clapped his right hand to his left shoulder, stood swaying for a moment, then sank to his knees.

Raglan holstered his gun and turned away, and behind him Lefty Greer lifted his voice in a great shout: "Tomahawk—Tomahawk!"

Raglan faced about. He saw Jake Leach come staggering from the saloon followed by two other Tomahawk men. Leach took up the same cry: "Tomahawk!" And suddenly men belonging to that outfit came running from half a dozen parts of the town. Raglan went on, running now.

Somebody else shouted, "Tomahawk!"

It was like a war cry.

And now they came after him, most of the Tomahawk crew.

CHAPTER ELEVEN

He stopped behind a farm rig and looked back. Half a dozen men were running along the street, guns drawn. Four others had taken to their horses, and now they overtook and passed their unmounted companions. Raglan glanced one way and another, seeking a way out. He was directly opposite Leyton's general store, and he darted across the street toward its open doorway.

A gun threw a flat blast of sound toward him, but the slug went far wide of its mark. He passed a group of women and children in front of Leyton's, sensing their panic. He rushed into the store, dodging past merchandise-stacked counters and customers. He kept on through the store to a stock room at the rear, and across it to the back door of the building. He saw the dark bulk of a barn standing some distance from the rear of another building, and sprinted toward it. A gunshot crashed, and this time he heard the shriek of the slug.

The man who'd fired at him shouted, "Here, Tomahawk!"

Raglan swerved away from the barn, plunged into an alleyway alongside the Bennett House. He fled through to the street, and voices shouted somewhere behind him. He crossed the main street at an angle, still running, and a yell lifted: "There he goes!"

He plunged into the yard of the Acme Freighting Company, working his way through the dozen or so wagons there. He came next to the Barton Brothers Lumber Company, entering the maze of stacked lumber. Behind him riders milled about in the wagonyard, and, since his pursuers had lost sight of him, he had a respite. He halted, leaning against a stack of boards, badly winded.

A gun racketed over at the side of town he had left, over behind the hotel, and the shot drew the mounted Tomahawk hands away from the wagonyard. They would return, Raglan knew, as soon as they learned that the shot had not been fired at him. But he had a few minutes in which to make his next move. He no longer thought of finding Lew Harnish. His concern now was not to clear his name but to stay alive, and he could do that only by escaping from Bennett. He had to get his horse from the livery stable.

He left the lumber yard, passed the rear of several shacklike houses, crossed a weed-grown lot, and reached the tangle of corrals behind the stable. He moved along the side of the building, then halted at its front corner. He glanced around the corner and caught a glimpse of someone standing in front of the stable's entrance. He ducked back out of sight, but then, hearing the yells of the manhunters, he knew that he could not remain there. Gun in hand, he went around to the front of the Star Corral.

It was Laurie Dane standing there.

She had been peering toward the center of town, but now she turned toward him. Startled, then, seeing his gun, she exclaimed, "Ed, is it you the Tomahawk hands are hunting?"

He nodded jerkily, continuing toward the doorway.

"Don't go in there, Ed!"

He halted, his back to the stable wall. "Some of them inside, Laurie?"

"My father."

"Alone?"

"The hostler is with him."

"Does he know his crew is gunning for me?"

"I don't know," Laurie said. "I came here a few minutes ahead of him. But if he knows—"

He said, "Matthew Dane's not stopping me. He—"

He glanced along the street, saw the shadowy shapes of several riders coming from the business section. Behind these mounted men, as many more followed on foot. He started toward the doorway and saw Matthew Dane coming from the stable with two horses in tow. Dane knew, all right. The instant he recognized Raglan, he bellowed the now familiar cry: "Tomahawk!"

Raglan leaped at him, clubbing down with the gun. The barrel caught Dane at the left temple with such force that he was knocked to his hands and knees. Raglan caught up the reins of the nearer horse, a stocky sorrel, and swung to its saddle. He wheeled it about, narrowly avoiding bumping Laurie as she ran to her father, and raked it with his spurs.

A yell lifted behind him: "That's him!"

The mounted Tomahawk men came after him.

He kept the sorrel running hard along the west road until he saw the bridge across Rock Creek, then swung off it and aimed for a clump of trees along the creek bank. He reined in among the trees and dropped from the saddle. The Tomahawk riders loomed through the darkness, racketed across the plank bridge, raced on along the road.

Raglan waited, and shortly a second bunch of riders came tearing along the road. These were the men who had been hunting him on foot. He had a bad moment when they slowed their mounts at the approach to the bridge, but then they too went clattering across and soon were lost in the darkness.

He debated his next move, knowing that his best chance of surviving the manhunt lay in reaching his own range at Squaw Creek. The rough country offered a thousand places for a man to hide. But now, with Tomahawk between him and the Squaw, he doubted that he could get through to it. He had no idea how far they would go in that direction before realizing that he had given them the slip. But once the realization came, they would return and search for him here. He glanced at the sorrel and saw that Matthew Dane carried no rifle on his saddle. Raglan knew that if it came to a gunfight, a rifle would stand him in better stead than a handgun, and the thought brought decision. He mounted the sorrel and turned it north along the creek at a lope.

After perhaps a mile, he swung away from the stream and headed east. When the lights of Bennett were directly south of him, he slowed the sorrel to a walk and headed toward the town. He approached the Star Corral from the rear, halting a little distance from the place. He could see and hear wagons and riders leaving Bennett, and knew that the ranch and homesteader people were homeward bound. The exodus continued for perhaps half an hour, and one by one the business places, other than the saloons, went dark. When he no longer heard any creak of wheels or clopping of hoofs, Raglan rode toward the Star Corral. He had just reached the tangle of corrals behind the stable when he caught the sound of riders coming in from the west. He held in the sorrel, waited, and a minute later a bunch of horsemen passed the building and loped on toward midtown. In the darkness he couldn't identify any of them, but he took it for granted that they were the Tomahawk hands.

He waited a few minutes longer, giving them a chance to get off the street and into the Stockmen's Bar. Then he rode to the front of the stable. The hostler was hitching up a pair of matched grays to a yellow-wheeled buckboard, there by the doorway, and Raglan recognized the rig as belonging to Ladder A. The hostler glanced around, then stared with mouth agape.

Raglan said, "Keep quiet. Don't go yelling for Tomahawk."

He dismounted and left Matthew Dane's sorrel there. A lantern hanging from a post just inside the doorway cast a pale yellow glow through the stable, and Raglan went back the runway looking for the stall in which his gray had been placed. He saddled the animal and backed it from the stall. Mounting, he rode from the building. The hostler had finished hitching up the buckboard team and was now lighting his pipe.

Raglan said, "That's Frank Amberton's rig?"

"Yeah."

"Where is Frank?"

"Still in town. One of his Ladder A hands stopped by and told me to get it hitched up. Mr. Amberton should be along any minute."

Raglan nodded, and rode out the way he'd come. When he cleared the town, he headed north along the road for about half a mile and then climbed a little knob and halted among the trees atop it. He took out makings, rolled and lighted a cigarette. It was smoked short by the time he heard the Ladder A rig coming. He called, "Pull up, Frank," and started down from the knob.

Amberton slowed his team. "Who is it?"

"Ed Raglan."

Amberton stopped, and Raglan, coming alongside the buckboard, saw that his wife was with him. Clara made a point of not looking at him, letting him know that she no longer considered him a friend.

Amberton said, "Ed, are you out of your mind? You shouldn't be hanging around here, with Tomahawk gunning for you!"

"I know. But I wanted to talk to you."

"If it's advice you want, I'll give it to you. Make tracks, Ed. Put as much distance between you and Matt Dane as you can."

"Let him run me off this range, Frank?"

"You can't fight Tomahawk, Ed."

"I'm doing it," Raglan said. "But not through choice. I didn't pick the fight. Tomahawk did. And now one of that bunch has a bullet hole in him, and Dane has a sore head. But that's not what I wanted to talk to you about. You know I was framed, Frank?"

"That was my first thought when Clara told me about it."

"You didn't know about it until you got back from Cheyenne?"

Clara said, "I told you he didn't know. Do you have to make me out a liar?"

Raglan said, "Let Frank speak for himself, Clara."

Amberton said, "I didn't know."

"You didn't know about that attempt on my life over in the Hatchet Hills, either?"

"The answer is the same, Ed. Not until Clara told me."

"You're not in Dane's confidence?"

"Hardly. I'm friendly with him; but he keeps his own counsel. Besides, if he's the man who's out to get you, he wouldn't tell me his plans. He knows you and I were good friends. He'd figure that I wouldn't stand for his pulling anything on you."

Raglan could accept Amberton's word for that, at least. Matthew Dane did not need to discuss his plans with another rancher, nor ask for help. He made his own decisions and was powerful enough to act on them. But beyond that one statement, Raglan did not know how truthful his one-time friend was. A man who'd turned out to be a rustler might be a liar as well.

Raglan said, "I'm not letting this hang over my head, Frank. I'm no thief, and I won't be hounded as rustlers are hounded. One way or another, I've got to clear my name."

The team was acting up, eager to run. Amberton hauled back on the reins, said, "Whoa, there—whoa!" and then, "It won't be easy, Ed. How are you going about it?"

"Well, I'll never get Matt Dane to admit that he framed me—if he is the guilty man. But there's that Association detective, Lew Harnish. I'll work on him."

"You think Harnish had a hand in it?"

"I don't know. But he can tell me who pointed out that cow with the blotched brand—and I've got a hunch it'll turn out to be a Tomahawk hand who forged my RAG brand on Dane's orders."

"He'll be hard to get at, if he's a Tomahawk hand."

"Hard for me to get at, but not for you."

Amberton frowned. "What do you mean by that, Ed?"

Raglan folded his hands on his saddle-horn and leaned forward so he could see both their faces. He said, "I think Clara knows what I mean."

Clara gave him a spiteful look. "He means you've got to help him, Frank," she said. "He thinks he can scare you into helping him."

Amberton swore under his breath. "Is that it, Ed? You'll let it out that I'm the man you covered up for in that Will Vance business, if I don't help you?"

"Let's say that one good turn deserves another," Raglan said. "I kept quiet about your being a rustler, and now you should be willing to help me prove that I'm not one."

"What do you want me to do?"

"What I can't do for myself, now that Tomahawk is gunning for me. Find out from Harnish who pointed out that brand blotched cow, then get whoever it is to admit that he forged my RAG."

"And get Matthew Dane down on me?"

"Dane and everybody else would be down on you, Frank, if I'd told that Will Vance had been in your hire."

"All right, Ed. I'll do what I can."

Raglan smiled wryly. "Good. I knew I could count on you, old friend."

Amberton merely grunted in reply to that. He let his team out. Raglan watched the rig until the darkness swallowed it. Then, with a shrug, he turned his horse in the direction of Squaw Creek.

More often than not, the hour before dawn is the darkest of the night. It was that late when Raglan got home. He rode the last hundred yards with his gun in his hand, holding the gray to a slow walk, and peering into the darkness about his buildings. He had seen the Tomahawk riders return to Bennett after he'd given them the slip at Rock Creek, but it would have been possible for them to set out for his ranch while he talked with Frank Amberton. He circled his buildings without seeing anyone, however.

Still doubting that they would call it quits after only one attempt to avenge his shooting of Lefty Greer and gun-whipping of Matthew Dane, he got his blankets from the cabin and rode to the timbered slope behind his buildings. Midway up, he off-saddled, staked out his horse and spread his blankets. He lay quietly for a while, just thinking.

There was some good to Amberton's advice that he put distance between himself and Matthew Dane. He couldn't fight Tomahawk with any hope of staying alive. On the other hand, the odds were against his returning to Tulare Basin once he left it. If fear drove him away, fear would keep him from coming back. So he would not clear out. If Tomahawk came to Squaw Creek, he would run—but only far enough to place himself beyond reach of that outfit's guns. And when Dane's riders withdrew, he would return. He would be safe enough if he guarded against being taken by surprise.

He slept finally, and did not awaken until midmorning.

His first act on rising was to study the range and his ranch buildings. Seeing no riders, he rolled his blankets and saddled his horse. He rode down to his headquarters, watered the gray at the creek, and then left it ground hitched on a patch of grass near the cabin. He went inside, built a fire and made breakfast. After breakfast, he stepped outside for a look across the range and still saw no riders. Somewhat surprised that no Tomahawk riders had come after him, he mounted and headed toward the entrance to Squaw Gorge.

It was Sunday, and, he decided, the proper day to call upon a lady.

His spirits lifted when he thought of Christine Mallory. And he knew, deep within himself, that it was because of her that he would not leave this range.

It was about two o'clock when he reached the Mallory ranch. Christine sat on the porch of the house, on a rocking chair, knitting a ball of dark blue yarn into what appeared to be a sweater. She kept her needles busy even while watching him cross the yard. He reined in, tipped his hat back off his forehead, folded his arms on his saddle-horn, and smiled at her solemn face.

"What's troubling you, Chris?"

"You."

"I?"

She said gravely, "Pa told me about the goings-on in Bennett last night. I'm beginning to think you're not going to last long enough to build up a big outfit over there in Squaw Creek." She rested her needles. She stopped rocking. "Pa said those Tomahawk riders did their best to kill you."

"Their best wasn't good enough."

"They'll try again. You know that, don't you?"

He nodded, smiling. Christine was concerned about him. He found pleasure in that. He said, "They'll try again, but they'll have no better luck. They're not going to kill me, Chris. They're not scaring me off this range, either. I'm going to have that big outfit. Can you believe that?"

Their eyes met, and it seemed to Raglan that hers were suddenly bright with the same excitement that he felt.

But she said, "I only believe what I see, Ed Raglan."

"You wouldn't bet on me against Tomahawk?"

"I've seen what the big outfits can do to little men," she said. "I saw Luke Chronister hanging from that tree, remember."

"I keep trying to tell you that I'm not just another little man."

"And you still don't convince me," Christine said. "Ed, don't take chances. It's better to lose everything but your life. Don't risk getting killed for a dream. And that's all it can be, this thing of your having a big outfit one day—a dream. But I wish it could be more than that. I really do."

"Keep wishing, Chris."

Suddenly two little smile-dimples appeared on her cheeks. She said, "Don't talk like that. You'll make me think there is some hope."

Sam Mallory came from the house before Raglan could reply to that, and at the same moment Steve and Jess came riding in from the south. They came at a lope, swung across the yard and reined in before the house.

Christine said, "You two must have had a big night in town."

Jess said, "We've got news, bad news." Both he and Steve looked glum, and Jess's voice was harsh with anger. "Some Tomahawk hands rode into Bennett late last night. They bragged that they caught Bart Somers on their range and killed him in a gunfight."

Christine gasped, "Oh, no!"

Raglan swore under his breath. He'd known that Somers was risking his life in going to Tomahawk, but still the news jolted him.

Jess said, "That's not all. Take a look at this."

He pulled a paper from his shirt pocket and held it up for them all to see. It was a duplicate of the paper Raglan had taken off Luke Chronister's body, a piece of brown wrapping paper bearing a crudely drawn skull and crossbones and the numerals 3-7-77. The sign of the Vigilantes.

"Where did you get that?" Raglan asked.

"From old J. C. Pierce," Jess said. "He saw us passing his place and hailed us. He found this on his cabin door when he got home last night."

CHAPTER TWELVE

Like Raglan, the Mallorys had been shaken by the news of the killing of Bart Somers, whom they had known well and liked despite his being a rustler, but now that was forgotten. They stared at the paper with a sort of numbed fascination, as people sometimes stare at a poisonous snake, and Raglan sensed their fear.

He broke the silence, saying, "That old man is no rustler, and those Vigilantes know it." He turned to Sam Mallory,. "Can you believe Pierce is a thief?"

"No," Mallory said. "And I never believed Luke Chronister was one."

"The big outfits want to drive the little ranchers off this range," Raglan said. "They left this warning to scare Pierce out. If he doesn't leave, they'll hang him like they did Chronister—and hope it scares some of the rest of us enough to pull up stakes and move out."

Mallory nodded.

"Well, are we going to let them get away with it?" Raglan asked.

"Hell, no. I can't be scared away."

Raglan didn't mean that, and said so. "We've got to help old Pierce."

"Yeah. We'll get him to move over here for a while."

"That's no good, Sam. The Vigilantes will get him when he moves back to his own place again." Raglan's voice was harsh with anger. "The thing to do is show that crowd that none of us, not even an old man like J. C. Pierce, can be driven off his range at all." He leaned from the saddle, took the paper from Jess and crumpled it in his fist. "Here's our chance to hit back. If enough of us go to Pierce's place and set a trap, we may be able to smash the Vigilantes, once and for all."

Mallory cleared his throat nervously. "I don't know about that," he said. "We'd be asking for a fight with the big outfits. We'd be starting a range war."

"Sure, I know," Raglan said. "The big outfits band together, organize. But the little ranchers go down one by one. But why, Sam?"

Mallory tugged at his beard, frowned with thought. "I don't know the reason for it," he said. "It's just that we always kill our own snakes. Maybe it's pride. Maybe we're too proud to ask each other for help. I doubt if old J. C. expects us to help him."

"A damn fool pride, that."

"Yeah, but—"

"I'm going to give Pierce a hand," Raglan said. "Are you with me?"

"Would we have a chance, Ed?"

"If we get some of your neighbors to come along, we'd have a chance."

Mallory nodded. "All right. I'm with you." He looked at his sons. "You two shift your saddles to fresh mounts and go visiting. Get as many Hatchet Hills men to come to Red Butte as you can. If you can't get any—well, you come alone." He glanced at Raglan. "You want to start out right away?"

"We'd better," Raglan said. "It'll be dark by the time we get there, and the Vigilantes may show up tonight."

They rode out a half hour later, Mallory leading a spare horse under pack. Knowing that Pierce could not afford to feed them for any length of time, they had decided to take along a supply of provisions. The old man's ranch was located on a mesa between the hills and Red Butte, the latter a high, mile-long rock formation. It was closer to the main portion of Tulare Basin than any other small spread, and Tomahawk was Pierce's nearest neighbor. They reached the north end of the mesa shortly after nightfall, and Pierce's croaking old man's voice challenged them as they drew close to his buildings: "Name yourselves!"

"Sam Mallory, J. C."

"Who's with you?"

"Ed Raglan."

"All right. Come on in."

Pierce stepped from the barn as they rode into his yard. He had a rifle in the crook of his arm. "Expected visitors," he said. "But not you two. What are you doing out this way?"

"Ed figured we should stand by you," Mallory told him. "My two boys will be along later—with some others, I hope."

"It's not your fight."

"We figure it is. It looks as though the big outfits are out to clear us little men off this range, and they're using the Vigilantes to do it. You haven't been doing any brand blotching, have you, J. C.?"

"No. And that's the gospel truth."

"Then it's just that somebody wants you out of here."

"And I know who that somebody is," Pierce said. "Matthew Dane. About a month ago he came visiting, real friendly-like. He had a bottle of whisky along. He tried to get me drunk, but I was too smart for him." He chuckled. "I knew he wanted something. 'Beware of Greeks bearing gifts,' I told myself."

"What did he want?" Raglan asked.

"My ranch."

"He offered to buy you out?"

Pierce nodded. "He said he'd buy my cattle and pay me five hundred dollars more for my buildings. He claimed he wanted some good pastureland he could fence off and use for a purebred Hereford herd. He figured that this mesa would take only a little fencing to close it off from the open range."

"Now we know," Raglan said. "Dane is no longer satisfied with running Tomahawk cattle on open range. The main part of the Basin is getting too crowded to suit him. And since he can't run out the other big outfits, he's after the graze in the Hatchet Hills."

"And he aims to get it," Pierce said, "by having the Vigilantes hang us for rustlers." He clenched his gnarled fists. "I'll go out fighting, but I won't hang."

"Maybe you won't have to go out fighting, either," Raglan said. "Sam, let's put up our horses."

They carried their supply of grub into Pierce's cabin, then turned the horses into the corral and placed their saddles in the barn. Raglan offered to stand watch while the two older men rustled up a meal, and he took a sentry post by a cottonwood tree to the east of the buildings. There was a sliver of a moon, and he could see the dark bulk of Red Butte far across the mesa. The night was quiet, and not until nearly midnight did he hear a sound of riders. Then Jess Mallory came in with two other Hatchet Hills ranchers, Al King and Charlie Ward. An hour later Steve arrived with three others, Mike Acton and his son, Russ, and Red Larsen.

Half a dozen ranchers had refused to join in any fight with the Vigilantes, according to the Mallory brothers. The men who refused had argued that they'd had no trouble with the Vigilantes or the big outfits, and didn't want to ask for trouble. The others, the five who'd showed up, agreed with Raglan, Pierce and Sam Mallory that they had better fight now as a group, with some hope of winning, than to be jumped individually later on when there would be no chance of them standing off the big-outfit riders.

Raglan kept watch all that first night, and on the second, the others took turns standing guard. There was no alarm either night. As darkness came the third night, Raglan was sure that the Vigilantes would wait no longer. They would certainly come now to see if their warning had scared Pierce off his land. Raglan got a lantern from the cabin and gave it to the Mallory brothers, with instructions to ride out to Red Butte. If they sighted riders coming onto the mesa, they would light the lantern as a signal for the men at the ranch. Then they would trail the Vigilantes in and, if a fight broke out, fire on them from the rear.

It was an hour after nightfall when Sam Mallory, keeping watch by the cottonwood, called to Raglan. "You see it?" he asked. "Or are my eyes playing tricks on me?"

Raglan saw it.

A tiny glare of light against the dark shape of Red Butte.

"This is it," Raglan said. "Tell the others."

Mallory went to the buildings, and Raglan heard him telling Pierce and the others that the signal had been seen. They had worked out a plan of action. Mallory, Pierce and the two Actons were to fort up in the cabin. Raglan and the remaining three men would station themselves in the barn. This would catch the Vigilantes in a crossfire if it came to a fight. But they would try to reason with the intruders before opening fire, in an attempt to make them understand that from now on the little cattlemen were united and would resist every move made by the big outfits. Raglan was to act as spokesman.

He waited until he heard the drumming of hoofs, then headed for the barn. Crossing the yard, he called out, "They're coming, all right," and heard Sam Mallory's curt reply, "Let them come, damn them!"

He entered the barn, closed the door except for a two-inch crack of space that gave him a view of the yard. It was inky black within the barn, but after a minute or two his eyes became accustomed to the darkness and he could make out his three companions at the loopholes they'd cut into the wall. Of the three, he felt that only Red Larsen had any stomach for a fight. King and Ward were grumblers. They had been bellyaching about wasting their time at Pierce's ranch. Raglan had an idea that they were suffering from a lack of nerve.

He picked up his rifle and levered a cartridge into the firing chamber. "All set?" he asked.

Red Larsen said, "All set. Bring on your Vigilantes."

The next moment the quiet was shattered by the racket of a big bunch of horsemen coming in between the buildings. They milled about for a minute or two, then finally reined in facing the cabin in a line abreast. Thirteen of them. An unlucky number, Raglan thought, and had the hope that it would be unlucky for them, not for himself and his companions. They had masked their faces with neckerchiefs. He wondered why they hid their faces when they intended to kill the only man they expected to find here. Dead, Pierce certainly would not be able to identify them.

"Pierce! You there, old man!"

The voice was harsh, demanding. Raglan did not recognize it.

He called out, "Stay as you are. You're covered, the lot of you!"

There was a ripple of movement: men starting violently, twisting in their saddles to peer at the barn, drawing their guns.

But his words had got to them, and there was no attempt to rush the barn.

The man who had shouted for Pierce said, "Who are you?"

"Ed Raglan."

One rider swore obscenely.

Raglan said, "You, there. The one who yelled for Pierce. Ride over here—alone!"

For a moment none of the Vigilantes moved. They were frozen there, except for the nervous prancing of some of their mounts. Then the leader of the band said, "All right, Raglan," and backed his horse out of the line. He swung it around and rode toward the barn. "Have your say, damn you!"

"Show your face."

"To hell with you!"

Raglan's rifle was leveled, its barrel protruding from the narrow crack between the edge of the door and the doorjamb. He squeezed the trigger, and the slug snatched the man's hat from his head and dropped it to the ground behind him. Raglan jacked another cartridge into the firing chamber.

"The next shot will be even closer."

"I told you—"

Raglan fired again. The Vigilante yelped and clapped his left hand to the upper part of his right arm where the slug had creased him. Raglan said, "Show your face," and worked the Winchester's lever once more.

Red Larsen called out, "Better do as he says, bucko." He fired a shot that caused the Vigilante to flinch visibly. Several other riders swung their horses about, but Sam Mallory shouted from the cabin, "Stay as you are!"

The man facing the barn pulled his neckerchief down from his face, and despite the darkness, Raglan recognized him: Hank Mockridge of the Double M outfit.

Raglan pushed the door open farther. He stepped outside. "That's better, Hank," he said. "I like to know who I'm talking to." He kept Mockridge beaded with his rifle. "Is Matt Dane with this bunch of bravos?"

"That's for you to find out, Raglan."

"I guess I know. If he was along, he'd be doing the talking."

"Smart, eh, Raglan? Real smart, you!"

"Aimed to hang old Pierce, did you?"

"There's got to be an end to this rustling."

"An old man like him a rustler? You loco, Hank?"

"There's evidence."

"Evidence like that hide with my RAG brand forged on it?" Raglan said. "Hank, you're playing Matt Dane's sneaky game. He tried to buy Pierce out not long ago. He wants this mesa. So he has Pierce framed as a rustler, for you Vigilantes to hang. If you'd got that far, Dane would have taken over this mesa and fenced it off—for Tomahawk. And then he'd have laughed up his sleeve at you fool Vigilantes."

"Talk's cheap, Raglan. You can make anything sound good, if you're handy with words."

"I wanted to be reasonable. Would you rather have gun talk?"

"You've got the whiphand. Crack the whip."

"It's up to you," Raglan said, stepping back to the barn doorway. "If you want to try and take Pierce, go ahead. We'll empty a lot of saddles. But if you don't want to fight, ride out—and don't come back. I'll give you fair warning, Hank, since you seem to be the leader of this crowd. I'm going to hold you responsible. If anything happens to Pierce in the future I'll come gunning for you.

"Anything more?"

"I've had my say. It's up to you now."

Mockridge stared at him for a moment, his face working. Then he wheeled about. "Come on," he shouted. "Let's get out of here!"

The others milled about, then followed him from the ranch-yard. The last to leave jerked his neckerchief from his face, twisted in the saddle to scowl at Raglan. It was the Tomahawk hand, Jake Leach.

"We'll be seeing you, Raglan!"

Raglan's companions came from cabin and barn, laughing loudly, slapping each other on the back. Old Pierce tried to dance a jig. Raglan took no part in the celebration. He watched the departing Vigilantes, thinking that it had been too easy. He heard Jake Leach yell something, then saw the entire band come wheeling about.

He shouted, "Watch it, watch it!"

And the Vigilantes opened fire.

CHAPTER THIRTEEN

Above the racket of gunfire, Raglan heard a man behind him cry out and another curse. He sensed rather than saw that those two had gone down. He had his rifle at his shoulder now, and fired into the bunched riders charging at him. He saw one rider topple from his horse, another reel in the saddle. He realized that he alone was trying to stop the attack. His companions—except for those shot down—were running for cover.

For a moment he was sure that this was the end for him and the others. Then two guns opened up behind the Vigilantes—the Mallory brothers' guns—and the attackers wavered. He stood his ground and drove two more shots at them. They swerved away. They swung over to the rear of the cabin, then, running their horses, circling widely to get out of bullet range. A few last shots came from their guns, and were answered by the Mallorys' six-shooters. Raglan ran past the cabin and fired another shot after the band. He tried again, but his Winchester was now empty.

They fled across the mesa in the direction of Red Butte, and were lost to him in the darkness.

He stood there a moment, blaming himself for not having foreseen that the Vigilantes wouldn't pull out without making a fight of it. He heard Jess and Steve Mallory ride into the ranch-yard. He returned there, and Jess, already down off his horse, struck a match and lighted the lantern they'd used to signal the approach of the night riders.

Steve also dismounted, awkwardly. He had a bullet wound in his left side. Two men lay face down, and in the yellow glare of the lantern Raglan saw that one was old J. C. Pierce and the other Al King. Sam Mallory knelt by King, rolled him over onto his back. King groaned, struggled to rise, and managed to sit up with Mallory's help. The left side of his face was bloody. Mallory called to Jess to bring the lantern closer, so he could examine the wound.

"A bad crease, is all," Mallory said. "Al, you'll be all right."

He went to Pierce, rolled him over, then instantly straightened. Nothing could be done for the old man. J. C. Pierce had been hit twice, between the eyes and in the center of the chest.

Sam Mallory said, "A hell of a lot of good we did here."

He said it to Ed Raglan, and the others looked at Raglan. Their sudden ill temper was something he could feel. It had been his idea to stand by Pierce, and now they were blaming him.

He said, "All right. So we got the worst of it. But I still think we did the right thing. The old man had friends with him at the end, at least."

Charlie Ward said sourly, "It's only luck that we're not all dead with him. Me, I'm getting out of here before that crowd comes back. And I'm taking Al with me."

They were all eager to leave, and suddenly Raglan understood the single outstanding bitter fact about these raggedy-pants ranchers. They had been little men too long to resist anything bigger than themselves. One setback and they were whipped. It would have been different if the Vigilantes had ridden out without a fight. That would have given these men a sense of power, a self-confidence. They had needed to feel that they could buck the big outfits. Now they would never know anything but defeat. Raglan thought bitterly that defeat was a natural thing for them.

They were not merely little men by the size of their outfits, but in mental outlook as well.

To hell with them, he thought. From now on, I go it alone.

He withdrew while they bandaged the wounds of Al King and Steve Mallory. He watched them saddle their horses. They ignored him until they were mounted, and then Sam Mallory said, somewhat sheepishly, "You coming, Ed?"

"Somebody's got to bury the old man."

"Oh, yeah. I guess we forgot about poor J. C."

"Go your way," Raglan said. "I can dig his grave."

"Well, if you don't need any help—"

"I don't," Raglan said.

Mallory muttered something about getting Steve home so his wound could be cared for, and the lot of them rode out. Raglan picked up the lantern and went into the cabin. He took a blanket off the bunk and returned to the yard to cover Pierce's body. He found a shovel in the barn, selected a spot behind the cabin, and began digging the grave.

At dawn he finished shaping the mound and erecting a small cairn to mark the grave. He went to the dead man's cabin, built a fire, made some coffee. He drank two cups of it, then had a smoke. The sun was beginning to rise above Red Butte when he stepped from the cabin. He'd forgotten that he had shot one of the Vigilantes from his horse during the brief fight, and was reminded of it upon seeing a shape lying in the grass just beyond the buildings. He stepped back inside for another blanket, then went out to cover the dead man.

It was Hank Mockridge.

He decided that there was some justice in Mockridge's death. He had told the man that he would come gunning for him if anything happened to J. C. Pierce, and since Mockridge had been leader of the Vigilante band, it was only fitting that he had paid for the taking of the old man's life.

He covered the body, knowing that the Vigilantes would return for it sooner or later. It was only proper that they should bury their own dead. He got his saddle from the barn, roped his gray in the corral and saddled it. Mounting, he rode into the pen and chased Pierce's three horses out onto the range to shift for themselves.

He struck out across the mesa, heading north toward Squaw Creek.

It was growing dark when he reached his own place, and again he rode in warily. No one was waiting there in ambush, but someone had been there during his absence. Held to the cabin door with a rusty nail was a piece of brown paper and upon it, in bright red, was the now familiar sign of the Vigilantes.

In a fit of temper, he ripped the paper from the door, crumpled it into a ball and flung it to the ground. Then, getting himself under control, he picked it up and smoothed it out. He folded it, placed it into his jacket pocket along with the paper he'd removed from Luke Chronister's body and the one J. C. Pierce had found on his door. He was acquiring quite a collection of those Vigilante calling-cards.

I'll ram them down somebody's throat, he told himself. If I live long enough.

That somebody, he was convinced, had to be Matthew Dane.

But the immediate object was to take precautions, so that he did stay alive.

He made up his mind on the spur of the moment. He went into the cabin and made a pack of his provisions and camp gear, carried it outside and lashed it to the gray's saddle. Leading the horse, he set out for Squaw Gorge.

He'd never before ventured into the forbidding canyon at night, and did so now with some misgivings. But he managed to descend the treacherous rock wall without mishap, then found his way, in stygian darkness, through the torturous narrow end of the canyon with the thunderous roar of the falls pounding at him. Travel was difficult, and several times he was tempted to halt until daylight. But finally he cleared the most rugged stretch, and was able to move on without danger to himself or his burdened horse.

Just before midnight he reached the acre-sized bench midway through the canyon, and here, with the gorge wider, some light from the moon and stars filtered in. He turned across the bench and at the base of the overhanging canyon wall he made his camp. It had not occurred to him on his previous trips into Squaw Gorge that he would one day use this lonely place as a hideout. But then he had never imagined that he would let anyone drive him away from his ranch. It seemed that a man did not decide where he would stay. He was pushed one way and another by bigger, more powerful men.

He caught himself up short, realizing that he dared not let himself get into the habit of that sort of thinking. It was the sort of thinking that kept men like Sam Mallory and his neighbors whipped before they ever tried to fight. He wasn't whipped, and he didn't intend to be. He was hiding out, yes. But he would use his hideout as a base from which to fight. Actually, his situation had not become more critical because his name now graced the Vigilantes' list. He'd had the Tomahawk crew gunning for him, and now, having received the Vigilantes' warning, he still had Tomahawk gunning for him—plus the other big outfits.

He shrugged it aside for the time being, gathered brush and started a fire and cooked his first meal of the day. After satisfying his hunger, he rolled a cigarette and sat smoking by the dying fire. He was safe enough here in the gorge, he supposed. It seemed unlikely that the Vigilantes would suspect him of hiding in that no man's land—or come after him if they did figure he'd holed up there. But being safe was only a small part of it. He had to fight back, and he still had no plan of action other than the one he'd outlined to Frank Amberton. He must prove that Matthew Dane had framed him, and he could do that only through Lew Harnish, the Association's detective, and the man who'd pointed out that cow with his forged RAG brand blotting out the Tomahawk brand.

Amberton had agreed to help him, to get in touch with Harnish.

His next move then, was to see Amberton and find out if he had kept his promise.

Fair enough. He would do that.

He left Squaw Gorge by its western end, so as to avoid his own range. It seemed important that he keep away from his ranch. The Vigilantes might be watching for him, and he did not want them to see him coming from the gorge at the eastern end. His one chance lay in keeping his hideout camp a secret. After leaving the gorge, he rode through the rock hills and dropped down into the little valley where the Mallory ranch was located.

Sam Mallory and Jess were talking to a man Raglan did not know, over by the barn. He nodded to them and rode on to the house. Christine appeared at the door as he reined in.

"How's Steve, Chris?"

"As well as can be expected."

"His wound isn't too serious, is it?"

"He'll live," she said. "He'll be himself in a few days, I suppose. But it seems to me any gunshot wound is serious. I keep thinking how close he came to being killed."

He frowned at her in a troubled way. "You too, Chris?" he said. "Do you blame me for what happened at Red Butte, like the others do?"

She regarded him levelly. "It's not that," she said. "If you really tried to help old Mr. Pierce. But I'm wondering if you hadn't some other idea."

"I don't get you, Chris. What other idea?"

"Maybe you'd better hear what Will Langley has to say."

Raglan glanced at the three men over at the barn. The Mallorys, father and son, were looking at him uncertainly. The stranger stared at him with genuine hostility.

"That's Langley?"

"Yes."

"Who's he?"

"He claims that Bart Somers and he were good friends, that they were camping back in the hills together before Bart went to Tomahawk and got killed."

"That means they were rustlers together."

"Whatever it means," Christine said, "you'd better hear what he has to say."

"I'll do that," Raglan told her, and in a sudden ugly mood swung his horse about and crossed to the barn. He reined in facing the three, but looking at Langley and not liking what he saw. "What's this you're saying about me, friend?"

Will Langley was a lean man with a sandy mustache and eyes of such light a gray that they seemed as chill and hard as bits of ice. He wore his gun at his left side with the butt front, for a cross draw. Langley was smoking a cheroot, and he talked around it.

"Maybe it's something you don't want to hear, Raglan."

"Don't worry about hurting my feelings."

Langley took the cheroot from his mouth and flicked the ash from it. "There's talk in Bennett that your feud with Tomahawk is just a cover-up."

"A cover-up for what?"

"For your being a snoop like Lew Harnish for the Tulare Basin Cattlemen's Association. According to the talk, you and Matt Dane worked out this scheme so you could get in with us Hatchet Hills cattlemen—and then cross us up."

Raglan's face hardened. He now understood what Christine had hinted at: that he had tried to lead the Mallorys and their neighbors into a trap at J. C. Pierce's ranch. He said, "You sure you didn't dream all this, Langley?"

"I sleep sound," Langley said. "I never dream."

"All right. So you heard it. Where?"

"From somebody who heard it in McDade's. But a man could hear it from most anybody in town. It leaked out from a floss in the Stockmen's Bar, one of the percentage girls who's friendly with Lew Harnish. She heard it from Harnish."

"Smart," Raglan said. "Damn smart."

Langley puffed on his cheroot. "What's that?" he said.

"It's smart of Harnish. He's spread just the kind of talk somebody like you would believe. He found out that I was banding some of the Hills ranchers together, and he had to queer that for me. And he's queered it with no trouble at all to himself or the men behind him." Raglan looked at Sam Mallory. "You believe it?"

Mallory shook his head. "I don't know, Ed. I just don't know."

"If I was working with Harnish, I wouldn't have done any shooting the other night at Pierce's ranch. Except for Jess and Steve, I was the only one who did any shooting. It was my gun that killed Hank Mockridge. Figure it out for yourself, Sam."

Langley said, "We've got only your word for it that it was your gun that downed Mockridge. The way Mallory tells it, that whole bunch of Vigilantes was doing a lot of wild shooting. Maybe one of his friends killed Mockridge by mistake. You can't talk your way out of this—or out of your part in the killing of Bart Somers."

"So I'm to blame for that too, am I?"

"It looks that way to me."

"Keep talking, Langley."

"Sure, I aim to," Langley said. "I was camped out with Bart. He said he was going to visit the Mallorys. When he got here, he found out from them that you were over in the Squaw Creek country. He told them he'd ride over to see you—to thank you for getting the message to him about his name being on the Vigilantes' list. Later you told the Mallorys that he went on to Tomahawk to try to see Matt Dane's daughter. And the next thing we know, he's a dead man."

"You've got part of the story. The other part is that I warned Bart not to go to Tomahawk."

So you say.

"You're accusing me of telling Matt Dane that Bart was on Tomahawk?"

"He wasn't a man to get caught by chance."

"He was, or he wouldn't have ridden to Tomahawk," Raglan said. "He asked for trouble. His going there was a fool stunt, and it's not hard to believe that some Tomahawk riders spotted him."

Langley dropped his cheroot to the ground, deadening it with the heel of his boot. "I don't believe it," he said. "I figure Bart would still be alive if somebody hadn't tipped off those Tomahawk riders. And since you were the only one who knew he was going to Tomahawk, that somebody must have been you.

You'd better head back to Squaw Creek, Raglan, and stay there. You've got no friends down this way."

Raglan glanced from him to the Mallorys, and he saw no friendliness now on either the face of Sam or of his son. They were the jury, they'd heard the case against him—and they doubted his innocence. And there was Christine too, over in the house, at least half convinced that he was what Langley claimed. It hurt, but he also felt a savage rage.

He said, "All right. Believe what you want—and from now on go it alone." He swore bitterly. "When I got home from Pierce's ranch, there was a Vigilante warning tacked to my door. I'm a marked man, just as Chronister was and old Pierce and Bart Somers. One of these days you'll be on the Vigilantes' list, Sam. But then you buck that crowd alone, too. And go down like the others. I'm the one man who would have stood by you. Yeah, and I'm the one man who knows how to fight that crowd. But you have to believe this lie put out by Lew Harnish!"

Mallory's bearded face worked painfully. "Ed, I don't know what to believe," he said. "You've got to admit—"

"Sure. I've got to admit that it looks bad," Raglan cut in. "And my claiming none of it is true doesn't make it look any better." He looked at Langley standing there with his thumbs hooked in his gunbelt and his eyes frostier than ever. "Since you believe I tipped off Tomahawk and got Bart killed, maybe you want to pay me back for that."

"Ride out, mister," Langley said. "I told you you've got no friends here."

Raglan stared at him for fully a minute, then lifted the gray's reins and turned it away. From the corner of his eye he saw Langley's right hand reaching for his gun. He hauled hard on the reins, turning the gray the other way, at the same time jabbing with his spurs. He drove the horse against Langley just as the man completed his cross draw. The animal's left shoulder struck the man in the chest and sent him reeling back against the wall of the barn. Langley swore and swung his gun up to club the horse across the head. The blow missed as Raglan reined the gray away and, as he followed through with his hard swing, Langley was thrown off balance. Raglan drew his right foot from the stirrup, kicked out and caught Langley under the chin with the toe of his boot. The man's head rocked back, and for a moment he was wholly defenseless. Raglan wheeled his mount about and swung from the saddle, dropping his weight against Langley's chest and driving him to the ground. He pinned Langley down, wrenched the gun from his hand, then rose. Langley lay gasping, the breath knocked out of him.

Raglan threw the captured gun onto the roof of the barn, then went to Langley's horse and took the rifle off its saddle. He threw it too onto the roof. He got back onto the gray and watched Langley pick himself up. The man still couldn't get his breathing under control. He stood swaying, making a sound of choking.

Raglan said, "Next time you try something like that on me, I'll pull a gun too. Remember."

He looked at the Mallorys. He saw no friendliness in them.

He glanced at the house as he crossed the yard. Christine had gone inside.

He lifted the gray to a lope and struck out across the valley. Once again he knew what it was to feel alone in the world.

He rode through the next valley, the one where Luke Chronister had lived and died. He turned in the direction of Squaw Creek, intending to skirt that stretch of rough country on his way to Frank Amberton's Ladder A. It was midafternoon when he approached the range of bluffs separating his own range from the rest of the Basin. He intended to follow the bluffs eastward, and then, at their end, wait until nightfall to cross open country. But now he saw smoke rising from beyond the bluffs, a vast funnel of gray smoke against the blue sky. It rose from the location of his buildings, and he knew that they were burning.

Knew too that they had been deliberately set afire.

He rode to the jutting rocks and dropped from the saddle. It took him some minutes to find a slope that he could climb. When he gained the top of the bluff, he could see the burning cabin and barn about a mile to the northwest. The flames were leaping high, both buildings burning like tinder. He saw several horsemen heading toward the gap in the bluffs east of him. They were too far off for him to identify them, but he knew who they were.

Tomahawk men.

Matthew Dane's men.

He remained there watching his home burn to the ground, wanting to see it so there could be no doubt in his mind as to what his next move should be. His loss was not great when considered from a financial viewpoint. Indeed, his investment in money had been a small one. But he had built his house and barn with his own hands, and that had given them a certain value beyond mere dollars and cents. The men who'd set fire to the place had known that burning a man's home was the best way to break his spirit. But that, Raglan told himself, was a game two could play.

And when darkness came that night he rode not to Ladder A, but to Tomahawk.

CHAPTER FOURTEEN

At about nine o'clock Raglan reached the cluster of low wooded hills which bordered Drum Lake. He reined in upon the crest of one of the higher hills and from there could see the lights of Tomahawk headquarters about three miles to the south. He climbed down to rest his horse, and smoked a cigarette while he waited. He was calm enough for what he had to do; he had control of himself, and his rage was a well-reined thing backing up his resolve.

When his cigarette was smoked short, he dropped the butt and ground it into the dirt with his boot heel. He mounted and rode slowly down from the hills, and the lights of Tomahawk grew brighter and larger and took the shapes of windows. He came to a creek and forded it, and in the trees at its bank he tethered the gray. He went on afoot, aiming directly toward the big log-and-stone ranch house.

He moved without stealth, certain that no guards were posted about these buildings. Matthew Dane would feel safe in his own headquarters, with his gun-carrying riders no farther away than his voice would reach. The man would have no fear of an enemy coming here. So almost openly Raglan reached the rear of the house, then walked along the side of it. He did stop at the corner of the building for a look about the wide yard, but then, seeing no one, he moved boldly to the stone steps and climbed to the veranda. A hundred yards away was the crew's bunkhouse, its open door bright with lamplight. He went up to the door of the house, tripped the latch and pushed the door open. He stepped into the unlighted hallway and closed the door behind him.

He heard a voice from the parlor, Laurie Dane's voice, and then music from a piano. With the girl's music deadening the thud of his boot heels and the jingling of his spurs, Raglan crossed the plank flooring of the hall and stepped into the huge front room. Laurie saw him at once, and with a discordant crash the music stopped.

She said, "Why, Ed!" and stared at him with alarm.

Matthew Dane sat by the fireplace, his heavy face all the ruddier because of the heat and glare of the log fire. He had a cigar in one hand, a glass in the other. The cigar would be fine Havana, Raglan supposed, and the whisky the best bourbon. There he sat by his fire in his comfortable house, the high and mighty master of Tomahawk taking his ease—and, Raglan suspected, scheming how he would become master of all the Hatchet Hills range beyond Tomahawk.

He was not a man to be startled, and Laurie's low-voiced cry did no more than cause him to turn his head slowly. And the sight of Raglan merely brought a frown to his face. But then, as the seconds ticked away, the frown darkened into a scowl, and he said, "Well, Raglan, do you make a habit of walking uninvited into a man's home?"

Raglan said, "When the man has my home burned."

Dane straightened in his chair, looking as alert as a man of his bulk could. "What's that?" he said. "What's that you say, man?"

Raglan's smoldering gaze traversed the parlor. It was a luxuriously furnished room, with red Brussels carpet on the floor and draperies at the windows. The chairs and sofas were overstuffed and their coverings of plush. He saw fuel for a fire. He counted three lamps—one a hanging lamp, one a student lamp on a desk in a corner, one with a flowered glass shade on a center table. The lamp on the center table, Raglan told himself, was the one he would use.

He moved toward the table and halted by it.

Laurie turned on the piano stool with increasing alarm in her eyes. Dane also became aware of the resolution in Raglan's stance. He put glass and cigar down on the small table beside his chair. He got to his feet.

"What ails you, Raglan?"

"That's a fool question, coming from you."

"Now see here, my good man—"

"Quit that, Matt," Raglan said. "Quit using that tone to me. I don't work for you, so don't talk to me as though I'm a servant. I'm your equal, Matt. No, by God—I'm a better man than you when we're face to face like this and you can't call in your gunhands!"

Laurie said, "Ed—Ed!"

Raglan said, "Never mind, Laurie. Just keep out of it. This is between your father and me." He didn't take his eyes off the man, and he saw the beginning of concern in Dane's manner. There was a slowly healing gash at Dane's temple, a wound left by the blow of a six-shooter. Raglan said. "Or maybe you'd better take part in this, Laurie. You know Bart Somers is dead?"

"Yes, I know."

"You know he was killed by Tomahawk riders?"

"Yes, Ed."

"And that all he wanted on Tomahawk was to see you?"

"No. No, I didn't know that, Ed."

Raglan said, "A man was in love with your daughter, Matt, and he's dead because of you."

"He was a rustler, a thief."

"Maybe he was, but there was good to him—and now he's dead because of you." Raglan sucked in a deep breath. "But I'm not dead. You turned your riders loose on me but they couldn't kill me. You framed me with that cowhide with my forged RAG brand, but I'm not going to stay framed. You put my name on the Vigilantes' list, but I'm not going to quit until I've stripped the mask off the face of the last damn night riders. You had my buildings burned today, Matt—and, damn you, now it's my turn to do some burning!"

"Raglan, you're out of your mind. You're a crazy man."

"I'm crazy mad, Matt."

"I'll give you five minutes to get out of here," Dane said. "Then I'm going to call my crew—"

"You're not calling anybody," Raglan said.

Dane started toward the door. Raglan caught him by the lapels of his coat and threw him onto a sofa. Then he returned to the table and picked up the lamp. Dane guessed his intention.

"Raglan, I warn you—"

"My shack meant as much to me as this fine house does to you," Raglan said, and flung the lamp with all his might.

There was explosive shattering of glass. Oil splattered the wall and formed a spreading pool on the floor. The wick still burned in the lamp's wreckage, and suddenly it ignited the oil with a burst of flame. Laurie came off the piano stool, screaming. Her father shoved past Raglan, gained the doorway to the hall. A moment later he yanked the outer door open and began bellowing at the top of his lungs for his crew.

Briefly Raglan watched the swift spread of flames, and then he turned away. Coming from the house, he saw Dane hurrying midway across the yard toward the bunkhouse. Dane was still shouting, and several men came from the bunkhouse as Raglan pounded down the stone steps. Two of the Tomahawk men started toward him at a run, and one opened fire with his revolver. The shots were great blasts of sound in the night, and Raglan, swerving in abrupt flight, heard the shriek of the slugs.

They came after him, not shooting now but trying to run him down. He put the house between himself and them, however, and then sprinted for the thicket of trees by the creek. He reached the trees, and his horse. He jerked the reins loose from the scrub tree to which they were tied, and swung into the saddle. A yell rose: "There he is!" Two men, then three more, ran toward him. He drove the gray from the trees and across the creek, and had just gained the opposite bank when a gun blasted once, twice and a third time. With the third shot he felt the blow of a giant unseen fist. He reeled in the saddle, and was forced to grip the pommel to keep from falling. The gray kept on running, and when the next shots came Raglan was out of handgun range.

He rode to the hills surrounding Drum Lake, climbed to the crest of one of the highest uplifts. He pressed a hand to his left side and felt the blood seeping through his shirt and ducking jacket. He looked south, saw the ruddy glare blossom, and knew that the flames were still raging, still spreading. It was not something he could crow about; in fact, he felt suddenly disturbed about the rightness of what he had done. True, he was not so weak that he could not hit back nor was he a man who did not pay his debts. But this seemed less than fair, and indeed, considering the value of Dane's house with his own, he had paid the man back with far too much interest.

Still, it was done—and Matthew Dane had it coming to him. The score was far from equal, taking into consideration that he had stopped a Tomahawk bullet.

He moved his neckerchief and wadded it inside his clothing, against the wound, hoping it would stem the flow of blood. There was pain, knife-sharp pain, but that he could bear. It was loss of blood that might bring about the finish of him.

He watched the distant glare grow brighter, saw how it colored a vast portion of the night sky. He heard a bunch of riders not far off, traveling at a lope, and took it for granted that they were searching for him. Evidently Matthew Dane considered it more important to have him hunted down than to have his ranch hands try to save his house. He remained there waiting for the Tomahawk riders to put distance between themselves and him, and trying to decide his next move.

He needed help now. His wound required care.

There was a doctor in Bennett, but Tomahawk would learn about it if he went to town. The Mallorys? No, they were soured on him—and, anyway, he would not involve them with Tomahawk. He thought of Frank Amberton, the man he'd once considered his friend. But he could not ask Amberton to risk trouble with Tomahawk by taking him in, even if the man would do so. There was nobody. He was as alone as a man could be. He had nothing but enemies.

He turned once more in the direction of Squaw Gorge.

CHAPTER FIFTEEN

He made it before his ebbing strength was wholly gone. He never quite knew how he descended the canyon wall and found his way through the rocky maze that made the trip through much of the canyon a nightmare, but he made it. He was even able to off-saddle his horse when he reached the bench midway through the gorge. But he was done in then, and could only wrap himself in his blankets and hope that his condition would not worsen.

He slept, and woke afire with fever in midafternoon. He was tormented by thirst, but couldn't rise to go to the creek. When he could bear the torment no longer, he crawled to the water, drank and was sickened, and had not the strength to return to his camp. He lay in the shade of some bushes, and sank into a stupor. When he regained his senses, it was night and he was confused in his mind. Some minutes passed before he understood where he was, and why. He dragged himself to the water's edge, and drank again. The fever still burned in his veins, and in every fiber of him. He lay back, slept by snatches, was haunted by nightmares—or rather, by one nightmare.

It was always the same terrible dream: he was hunted like a wild creature, and everywhere he fled there were riders seeking to head him off, to ride him down, and every one of them resembled Matthew Dane.

He heard voices, and awoke screaming—and knew that the only voices were his own, in delirium, and that of Squaw Creek. Then in the gray dawn of the second day, he awoke and found himself drenched with sweat and shivering with the cold that knifed through to the marrow of his bones.

It was then that the fever broke, and he knew that the worst was past. He needed warmth now, a fire, hot coffee, his blankets. He managed to rise and take a few lurching steps toward his camp, then fell and had to crawl again. When he got across the bench, to the camp beneath the overhanging rock wall, he was unable to start a fire. He wrapped himself in his blankets and lay in the sun, and so spent the day and the night that followed.

The third day he was so weak that he trembled, but his mind insisted that he move from where he lay. He forced himself to crawl to where his gear and provisions were stacked, and he found some stale biscuits from the last meal he'd cooked—so long ago—and he wolfed them down. He made the trip to the creek again, crawling as before, but he was spent once more after he had drunk. He lay back and stared up at the brassy sky.

He was still lying there when, in early afternoon, he heard a clop-clopping of shod hoofs. He told himself that he imagined it, but the sound grew louder and insinuated itself into his mind. Admitting that a rider actually was in the gorge and approaching him, he experienced sudden fear but was too weak to sustain it. He lay waiting for the blast of the shot that would end it all.

It could be no one but a Tomahawk rider. And, as in his recurrent nightmare, it would be Matthew Dane.

"Ed!"

He opened his eyes and saw her there—Christine. He closed his eyes, then opened them again. She was dismounting, swinging down from the saddle of the stocky strawberry roan that he once had ridden. She came and dropped to her knees beside him. She made no sound of crying, but he saw tears come to her eyes and spill over onto her cheeks.

"Chris?"

"Yes, Ed."

"It's good to see you, Chris," he said. "It's real good to see you."

She did for him what he could not do for himself. She got him to his feet and, supporting most of his weight, walked him to his camp. She got a fire burning and cooked him a meal, and she fed it to him when his hands proved too shaky to lift the food to his mouth. It was the hot coffee that seemed to do the most good. Its warmth spread through him, and his sluggish circulation speeded up. His strength did not return immediately, but he no longer felt so shaky.

Christine was not finished doing for him. She heated water and cleaned his wound, and afterward helped him out of his clothes. While he lay wrapped in his blankets, she washed them clean of blood stains at the creek and spread them out on a boulder in the sun to dry. He had grown drowsy while she was at the creek, and shortly he slept. When he woke several hours later, it was as though he had made a miraculous recovery. He felt stronger, and his mind was clear. Christine sat nearby, watching him.

He rubbed a hand over his bristly face. His cheeks felt hollow under the wiry stubble. He said, "I must look like a wolf after a hard winter, Chris."

"I've seen you looking better, Ed."

"I guess I was pretty much a goner."

"I came along just in time."

"How did you happen to find me?"

She smiled. "That's a foolish question. I came looking for you. I decided there was only one place you could be, here in the

Squaw. I knew the Tomahawk riders were looking everywhere else, without finding you. And since I knew how you travel through here—well, I decided to come and see if you weren't hiding here. They were all through the Hatchets, Ed. They were at our ranch three, four times. They knew you were wounded. They mentioned that to us. That's why I decided to look for you. I knew that if they were right in thinking you were wounded, you would need help."

"How did you find your way into the Squaw?"

"I almost didn't. I turned back twice before I got down. I was scared out of my wits, even after I got down the canyon wall. But I kept telling myself that if you could get in and out of it, I could too."

"But why, Chris?"

"Why did I come?"

"The last time I saw you, you believed I was what that Will Langley said."

Her eyes clouded. "I admit that, and I'm ashamed. But that was right after Steve was wounded, and Al King, and old Mr. Pierce was killed. I was so upset that—well, I would have believed anything of anybody. Or maybe I didn't really believe such a thing about you, Ed. Not deep inside me." She fell silent a moment, then added, "I suppose at the bottom of it, for all us Mallorys, there was the suspicion that no one—you or anybody else—would really quit a big outfit and go back to being a raggedy-pants cattleman. We talk proud a lot of the time, but we're really envious of the big outfits. It's a hard life, Ed, the way we live. So when Will Langley told us you were still working for that crowd secretly, it seemed possible to us. But we knew different, when those Tomahawk riders came into the hills looking for you."

"They didn't get tough with you Mallorys, did they?"

"No. They tried something else. They told us that Matthew Dane would pay a thousand dollars to the person who led them to you."

"So he's put a bounty on my hide."

"What did you expect, Ed, after burning his ranch house?"

"That was a fool stunt, I guess."

"Whatever possessed you?"

"His riders burned me out," he said. "They didn't mention that, I suppose."

"No, they wouldn't tell what they'd done to you," she said. "Are you sure Tomahawk riders burned your place, Ed?"

"It couldn't have been anybody else."

"Vigilantes, maybe."

"One and the same," he said. "But the Vigilantes ride by night, with their faces masked. My buildings were burned in broad daylight. By Dane's men, Chris. They've been hounding me ever since Dane framed me with that damn brand blotched cow. They beat me up, and they tried to gun me down. Why would they shy away from burning me out?" He lay there feeling his rage return. "Matthew Dane wants me dead or driven off this range. He's wanted that since the night of the party at Tomahawk when I talked up against his Vigilantes."

"You're right, of course," Christine said. "But, Ed— what now?"

"I won't be driven off."

"Then sooner or later they'll kill you."

"Would you want me to let them scare me away?"

Christine said huskily, "I don't want you to be killed, Ed. Don't you know that?"

He stared at her, and understanding came to him in a sudden burst of knowledge. This girl had risked her life to come into Squaw Gorge seeking him. She would have done so much for no other man, and he should have realized that from the moment he opened his eyes and saw her there. He said, "Chris."

"Yes, Ed?"

"When did this happen?"

"I don't know exactly," she said. "Maybe the day we met at Luke Chronister's place. I hated you then for being a big-outfit man, but I couldn't forget you. I kept thinking about you. Then after you came to our place that day with the message for Bart Somers, I had you in my thoughts even more. I thought about you differently than I'd ever thought about another man. I wondered what it would be like to be—to be—" She faltered, flushing hotly.

A smile lighted Raglan's gaunted, unshaven face. "That's what I wanted," he said. "To have you wonder what it would be like to be my girl."

"I know. I saw it in your eyes when you looked at me."

"I'm luckier than I deserve, Chris."

"Lucky? You?" She shook her head. "I want to be glad about this, but I feel like crying. How will we ever have each other, Ed, if you go on fighting Tomahawk—if you're killed by Tomahawk?" She moved closer, bent over him, took his face between her hands. "Ed, do it for me. Please!"

"Run?"

"That's the sensible thing, Ed. And no one could blame you."

"I'd blame myself," he told her. "Remember my saying once that I was different from the other two-bit cattlemen? I meant it. I'm not running and leaving behind my Squaw Creek range and my cattle and my hopes for the future."

"It's better to be alive and have nothing."

"No. Then I wouldn't even have you."

"I'd come to you," Christine said. "Just send for me when you're safe."

"I couldn't," he said. "I might be safe, but I'd have to go back to working for a cowhand's wages. If I'm to have you at all, I want to know that one day I'll be able to give you a better life than you've had. Besides, if I let myself be whipped on this range, I'll let myself be whipped wherever I go—by any man who gets the notion he wants to push me around. I'm sorry, Chris, but I'm staying. I've got to stay."

She drew away, nodding. "I guess I understand, Ed." She forced a smile. "At any rate, I won't quarrel with you about it." She stood up. "I'll go now. Pa and the boys have no idea where I am, and I don't want to stay away so long that they'll worry. You won't do anything foolish while I'm gone?"

"You're coming back?"

"Of course."

"I'll be here," he said. "I'm in no shape to do anything foolish."

"There's one thing bothering me. What if Tomahawk comes down here?"

He chuckled. "Nobody goes down into Squaw Gorge," he said. "Nobody's that loco. Nobody but you and I."

She patted his hand and went to her roan horse. She saddled it as quickly and deftly as a man would have done, but her every movement was unconsciously feminine. She rose lithely to the saddle then, entirely a woman despite the fact that she wore mannish riding clothes and rode astride. She held the roan in for a minute, looking at him. He saw her against the sky, her hair coppery bright against the blue, and he fell in love with her all over again.

She said, " 'By, Ed," and wheeled the roan away.

He listened to the fading hoofbeats, but felt no loneliness now that she was gone. He would never know loneliness again. But he marveled that she should feel toward him as he felt toward her. He was no bargain at the moment for any woman, let alone a girl as wonderful as Christine Mallory.

CHAPTER SIXTEEN

He rose as dusk came to the canyon, putting on the clothing Christine had washed for him. He moved about for a few minutes, but his legs were wobbly and he soon had to rest. He kindled a fire then, and made coffee. He drank it hot and black, and ate the remainder of the food she had cooked. He would have liked to keep the fire, but some Tomahawk riders might come to the rim of the canyon and see its glare. Or some Hatchet Hills men who knew of Dane's thousand-dollar bounty offer, and might want to collect it. He had kept it from Christine, but he was afraid that someone would sooner or later decide that he was hiding in Squaw Gorge. At nightfall, he turned in and instantly fell asleep.

He awoke at dawn, and was surprised by the change in himself.

He wanted to get up and about, and, though he found himself still shaky, he pulled on his boots and walked to the creek. He returned to the camp, started a fire, cooked breakfast. After eating, he got razor and soap and returned to the creek. He lathered up and scraped the heavy stubble from his face, thinking of Christine as he wielded the razor.

She was in his thoughts almost constantly during the day, but it passed without her returning, and his disappointment was great. The following day was much the same. He kept expecting her, looking for her, but again she did not come. But now he knew that she had some good reason for staying away. He could guess at the reason: Tomahawk riders were nearby, and she was afraid that she might lead them to his hideout.

Still, if Christine did not return, his strength did. His wound was no longer troublesome; it had begun to heal. He kept busy, moving about, cutting brush for kindling, cooking and eating his meals. He was helping himself get his strength back. That second day he must have overdone it, for by nightfall he was done in and glad to bed down.

She came the third day, about noon. And when he saw her, Raglan felt a sudden alarm. He told himself that he shouldn't have let her come down into the gorge a second time, as dangerous as the trip was. But she had made it safely, and her face lighted up with pleasure when she saw that he was so far recovered that he could come to meet her. She reined in and dismounted.

"You look more like your old self, Ed."

"A few more days, and I'll be my old self," he said, and took her in his arms. "I missed you, Chris."

"I'm glad you did," she said. "But I didn't stay away to find out whether or not you would miss me. Ed, I've been to Tomahawk."

He stared at her. "To Tomahawk. Why, for Pete's sake?"

She moved away, seating herself on a boulder at the creek bank. She pushed her hat back and let it hang at her shoulders by its chin strap, freeing her hair to the sunlight. "After I left you the other day, I kept thinking what you told me about Matthew Dane—how he was at the bottom of all your trouble."

"Go on, Chris."

"Well, I had some idea of appealing to him. Maybe I thought if I pleaded with him, he would end this crazy business. Or maybe I thought I could get his daughter to help me with him." She smiled at his astonishment. "We hit it off fine, Laurie and I."

"But not you and Matthew Dane, I'll bet."

"He did give me a hearing, Ed."

"Oh?"

"I listed your grievances against him," Christine said. "That you accuse him of having you bushwhacked after the party at Tomahawk, and of framing you as a rustler."

Raglan hunkered down before her and took out makings. "And he denied it?"

"Yes, he did."

"Well, he would," Raglan said, and rolled and lighted his cigarette. "Why should he admit it?"

"Ed, I believe he told the truth."

"Chris, a man just doesn't admit such things."

"A man like Matthew Dane would. You know why? Because he's not afraid of anything on earth. You sense that when you talk to him."

"You're right about that. Matt Dane's not afraid of the Devil himself."

"He was willing enough to admit what steps he did take against you."

"Yeah? What steps were those? As if I didn't know."

"He admitted using his influence to have you fired from your job at Seventy-seven Ranch," Christine said. "And to turning his crew loose on you after you burned his house."

"That's all he admitted?"

"He said his riders had made trouble for you on their own. He said he'd given them no orders to molest you. Ed, it's your burning his house that he really holds against you. I think he's half convinced that you were framed."

"But, damn it, his men burned my buildings!"

"He claims they didn't."

"Chris, Matt Dane fooled you," he said. "He pulled the wool over your eyes."

Christine said, "I don't believe he did, Ed. It's somebody else working against you. You must have an enemy you don't know about. Ed, did you ever have trouble with any other of the big-outfit men?"

That jolted him. He rose and paced to and fro, agitated. "Chris, maybe I've been a blind fool," he said, halting before her. "There is somebody else, but I—well, I just wouldn't let myself suspect him. I was so sure it was Matt Dane—after all, a Tomahawk cow was used to frame me—and I didn't give this other man any thought."

"Who is it, Ed?"

"Frank Amberton."

"Of the Ladder A?"

"Yeah."

"What does he have against you?"

"I caught a mavericker named Will Vance burning Amberton's Ladder A on a Seventy-seven cow," Raglan said. "I let Vance go, told him to clear out of the country. I meant to cover up for Amberton."

"Why, Ed. Why?"

"We used to be good friends, Amberton and I."

"You told him that you caught Vance?"

He nodded. "The night of the party at Tomahawk," he said. "I talked to Frank, warned him to watch his step. I knew he must have had more maverickers than Vance working for him. Later, when the Vigilantes' meeting was called, I lost my temper and blurted out that I'd let Vance go because I was covering up for a big-outfit man. That must have scared Amberton. Yeah—and so he decided to fix me so I could never give him away."

"He could have bushwhacked you that day in the Hatchets, then?"

"More likely it was somebody he hired to kill me."

"And when that failed, he framed you so you'd be discredited among the big outfits. And if you named him as a rustler nobody would believe you."

"Chris, I've been a damn fool," he said bitterly. "It's clear enough now. It must have been Amberton, not Dane. And all the while I thought our friendship meant as much to him as to me. Hell, I'd never have given him away. He should have known that." He laughed, mirthlessly. "I even went to him for help!"

Christine regarded him curiously. "What did he say? How did he act?"

"He wasn't home when I went to Ladder A. I saw his wife. I'd known Clara before Frank married her. She tried to explain why Frank had hired men to rustle cattle for him. She claimed they'd been reckless with money and were in debt. She said Frank knew nothing about the attempt on my life or my being framed. She—" He stopped abruptly, remembering how Clara Amberton had used her feminine wiles on him in an attempt to get him to leave Tulare Basin.

Christine said, "What, then, Ed?"

"Clara tried to get me to clear out," he said. "She worked hard at it. I should have been suspicious then. Later, the night Tomahawk tried to gun me down in Bennett, I saw her and Frank. I waited for them outside town. Frank tried to get me to leave the Basin, too. He promised to help me prove I'd been framed." Again he laughed shortly, harshly. "And I believed he would."

"Well, now we know," Christine said. "Frank Amberton is the man."

"Yeah. But what good does our knowing do?"

"There must be something you can do, some way to use the knowledge to save yourself."

He shook his head. "You're forgetting Tomahawk," he said. "I can't get at Frank Amberton because of Tomahawk. I'm still caught in a trap, because of my own blundering. Unless—" An idea came to him. "Matt Dane told you he didn't send his riders to burn my buildings, Chris?"

She nodded.

"But if they did burn them and I can prove it," he said, "I'll have Dane in a corner. I'll be able to justify my burning his house. Even if he didn't send his men to burn me out, he's got to take the blame for what they pull—if only because they're on his payroll. You see?"

"They may have been sent by Frank Amberton, Ed."

"I doubt it. Amberton knows he's got me in a jam, and he'd figure that Dane's crew and the Vigilantes, one or the other, would finish me off. He wouldn't bother to send his men to burn me out."

Christine said excitedly, "You may be right. But how can you prove it?"

"Is the Tomahawk crew still manhunting me in the Hatchets?"

"Yes. They've set up a camp just outside the hills."

"They don't travel together when they're hunting me, do they?"

"No. They ride by twos or threes," Christine said. "The last time they came to our place, when they told us about Dane's reward offer for you, there were two—Jake Leach and another."

Raglan puffed thoughtfully on his cigarette, then stubbed it. He looked grim. "Jake Leach," he said. "He's the man. He hates my guts, and he's the meanest one in the Tomahawk crew. He was with the Vigilantes the night they came to old Pierce's ranch. He told me then that he'd see me again. Chris, I'd gamble on it. Leach was the leader of the bunch that burned my buildings. Look, will you help me?"

"You know I will, Ed. But how?".

"I've got to get hold of Jake Leach."

"No, Ed!" she cried. "The danger—"

"It's my only chance," he cut in. "If I can prove that Dane's men burned my buildings, he'll have to admit I was justified in burning his house. Maybe he'll be fair-minded enough to call it quits. Then I'll be free to go after Frank Amberton. Chris, I am caught in a trap and this is the only way out."

"Ed, I'm scared!"

"All you'll have to do is get in touch with Jake Leach. Make him think you want to collect Dane's reward. You can fool him."

"I'm not scared for myself, but for you."

"You don't need to be," he said. "You'll catch Leach when he's separated from the Tomahawk crew, except maybe for a man or two. And down here in Squaw Gorge I'll be able to handle him and a couple more." He took her by the shoulders. "You've got to do it, Chris."

She said huskily, "All right, Ed," and then came into his arms.

She clung to him as though this would be their last time together, as though she was convinced that what she promised would be the end of everything for them.

CHAPTER SEVENTEEN

It was late afternoon when Christine reached the rim of the canyon, safely but with her heart hammering from exertion and fright. Despite what she'd told Ed, the trip down and back seemed more fearsome each time she made it. Today, climbing, leading her roan, she had slipped and almost fallen from a shelf of rock. Only her firm hold on the roan's reins had saved her from a drop of a hundred feet or more, to certain injury and possible death. She had been negligent, of course. Instead of being careful of her footing, she had been full of the memory of Ed's arms about her and Ed's lips upon hers. And she had been worrying, too, about what she must do. Not about her part in the plan, for she was sure she could cope with Jake Leach, but about the danger to Ed Raglan.

Once clear of the canyon, she rode at a steady lope and an hour and a half later arrived home. Her father and brother Jess had not yet come in off the range, but Steve, now nearly recovered from his wound, was lounging on the porch steps. He watched her put up the now blowing roan, and then asked, as she crossed the yard from the corral, "Where you been, Sis?"

"Just riding."

"Queer way to ride, back in the rock hills and toward Squaw Gorge."

She stopped before him. "What makes you think I rode that way?"

"The direction you came from," he said. "Over that north hill."

Christine hesitated, wanting to tell him about Ed and fearing to. The Mallorys were a closely knit family, clannish. None had secrets from the others. But she was still uncertain of how her father and brothers felt about Ed. Steve's rather homely face showed a sudden grin.

"How's Raglan getting along in his hideout, Sis?"

"Smart, aren't you?"

"Real smart. But you want to know something? You're not being smart. That Association detective, Harnish, rode by here this afternoon. Just after you rode out. If he'd caught sight of you, he might have trailed you right to Raglan."

Christine was frightened, and showed it. "But he didn't—"

"No. He headed west toward Al King's ranch."

"Steve."

"Yeah? What's bothering you?"

She again hesitated, then blurted out, "Steve, how do you feel about Ed? You can't still believe he's secretly working for the big outfits."

Steve reached out and rumpled her hair. "Ed's all right," he said. "Langley made Pa and Jess and me suspicious of him, but we got over it." He grinned at her. "And if you've picked him for your man, I reckon he's got to be all right with us. Is that all that's bothering you—what we think of Ed Raglan?"

"No, not all," she said, and then told him what Ed and she planned. She ended up; saying, "I'm scared it won't work, Steve. Once I lead Jake Leach to Squaw Gorge anything can happen. He may not go down alone or with only one or two men. He may go with the whole Tomahawk crew, and then Ed wouldn't have a chance."

Steve thought about it, but only said, "There's Pa and Jess coming. You'd better go get supper on."

She tried not to worry while cooking the meal and setting the table. When her menfolks came into the kitchen, she knew that Steve had told Jess and their father about her visit to Ed Raglan. She knew from the searching looks Jess and Pa gave her as they took their places at the table. As usual, nothing was said during the meal. Like all their kind, the Mallory men came to the table to eat and not to talk. But afterward, Sam Mallory pushed his chair back and sat lighting his pipe instead of leaving the table immediately. Her brothers still sat, too. Her father waited until she rose to clear the table, then pointed the stem of his old pipe at her.

"Daughter, you aiming to have Raglan for your man?"

Christine was accustomed to bluntness, but now her cheeks burned with embarrassment. She said, evenly enough, "He hasn't asked me to be his wife, but I'm counting on it—if he gets out of his trouble alive."

"All right, then. We're all in this with you."

"But—"

"I figure you've made a fair choice, Chris," Sam Mallory said. "Jess and Steve figure so. So we're going to help. Now where's he hiding out?"

Christine had to blink away tears, happy tears. "In Squaw Gorge."

Her father nodded. "So Steve said, but I didn't think it likely. You been in and out of there?"

"Yes, Pa. Twice."

"So it can be done, eh?" Mallory said. "You're aiming to take Jake Leach down into the Gorge, but you're worried that he'll take too many Tomahawk hands along for Raglan to handle. Well, like I said, we're all in this with you. We'll see to it that the odds ain't too big for Raglan to handle. When you going to see Leach?"

"Tomorrow," Christine said.

Sam Mallory chomped the stem of his pipe. "Busy day," he said, "tomorrow."

Raglan had no way of knowing if Christine would come with Leach that day or the next or at all. But he made ready. He breakfasted at dawn, then saddled his horse. He checked his revolver and rifle. At broad daylight, long before he could see the sun from the depths of the gorge, he mounted and rode from the bench into the narrowing west end of the Squaw. A mile from the bench, the going became difficult and he tethered the gray amid a brush thicket. He took his saddle gun and went on afoot. An hour of hard going brought him to a point where he had a view of the canyon's end. He sought a hiding place among some of the giant boulders that would permit him to keep watch on the rock wall. He put down the rifle and waited. He felt shaky.

It wasn't like him to be so on edge. Ordinarily, he was as steady under stress as a man could be. But there was still some weakness in him from his wound, and being forced to hide out, he had discovered, did something to a man's spirit. Too, so much depended upon the success of his scheme that fear of failure made him tense. The whole affair could end as a fiasco, so risky was his plan.

He wanted to get Jake Leach down in Squaw Gorge and somehow overpower him. He believed he could accomplish that provided the Tomahawk man did not bring more than one or two others with him. Once he had Leach disarmed and helpless, he would find a way to make him talk. All he wanted was an admission that Tomahawk men had burned his buildings, so he could go to Matthew Dane and point out to him that the two of them were now even Steven. It was his belief that Dane, for all his toughness, would agree that when a man's buildings were burned he was justified in doing some burning on his own. Dane wouldn't be able to shrug off his responsibility for the actions of his hired hands, when, orders or no orders, they were acting for their outfit, in his behalf. Maybe he was counting too much on Dane's fair-mindedness. Dane might not admit responsibility for what his men had done, and so refuse to call them off. But this was his only hope of escaping from the trap into which Tomahawk had driven him.

As the morning passed, Raglan's edginess increased and he began to worry that Christine would be unable to deceive Leach. It occurred to him that the Tomahawk hardcase might have learned of her visit to that outfit's headquarters to plead with Dane. If that were the case, Leach would not be deceived for a minute into believing that Christine meant to lead him to Ed Raglan's hideout. Rather, Leach's suspicions would be aroused and he might attempt to force her to tell what her game really was. Raglan's concern for Christine's safety made him more uneasy, and he silently cursed the desperation that had led him into involving her.

By midafternoon he was about convinced that Christine would not show up that day with Leach—if she showed up at all. Then suddenly a group of riders appeared at the canyon's rim.

Six riders.

Raglan felt a quick anguish, for he assumed that one was Christine and the others Tomahawk men. The odds of five to one were too many, even though the element of surprise would be his and he had a certain advantage in knowing the gorge and intended to make use of that knowledge. They were too far above for him to identify which was Christine and which was Leach, and for what seemed an eternity to him, as he crouched among the boulders, they remained there on the rim-rock. He could guess the reason for their reluctance to follow her down the treacherous wall. Suspicion would have come to Leach and the others by now, if it had not before, and they would want to know how Christine had learned that Raglan was in the gorge. Maybe they were demanding an explanation. If so, Christine would be hard put to find one. But a moment later one rider began the dangerous descent.

That would be Christine.

He found himself holding his breath as she started down. She quartered down a gravelly slope, and a small slide of dirt and rock fell away from under her horse's hoofs. But she made it safely to a ledge of firm rock and rode more easily. Next, on a lower level, she made a switchback. She was now about fifty feet below the rim of the wall where the other five still sat their mounts. She continued downward by a series of switchbacks, moving with painful slowness, and then, a fourth of the way down, she dismounted and led her horse. Raglan knew that she was now navigating the most risky portion of the descent, and he broke into a sweat as he watched. Then he sighed with a vast relief as she left the narrow shelf of rock and got back into the saddle. She was now halfway down, and the remainder of the slope was less difficult.

Raglan was so intent upon the girl that now, looking upward, he was surprised to see that a second rider had started the descent.

That would be Jake Leach, he hoped.

Leach, if it were he, took it even more slowly than Christine, and perhaps fifteen minutes passed before he reached the shelf and dismounted. By that time a third rider had left the rim, and a minute later a fourth started down. Shortly two more riders appeared above, and at sight of them Raglan's heart sank. The odds were far too great, and the sensible thing for him to do was to retreat. He should withdraw to where he had left his horse, ride to the eastern end of the gorge and climb from it there. That meant deserting Christine, but he supposed that, when Leach saw his abandoned camp on the grassy bench, the Tomahawk man would assume that she had kept her part of the bargain, and was not to be blamed that their quarry had fled.

He was reluctant to leave, however, for once he started his flight he would not dare stop, unless he wanted to risk a suicidal showdown with Tomahawk. If he ran, he would have to keep running until he was clear of Tulare Basin. He put the thought of flight from his mind and reached for his Winchester. The showdown would be here, in Squaw Gorge.

Christine was down from the canyon wall, out of sight among the maze of rocks and tangle of brush between him and it. The second rider had come more than halfway to the bottom, while the third and fourth had halted at the shelf which they would have to travel afoot. They seemed frozen there, and Raglan hoped that they'd lost their nerve. He looked upward, to the canyon rim, and was astonished to see that the remaining four riders were turning away from there. His spirits lifted. It appeared that there would be no odds, after all.

He had an occasional glimpse of Christine now, working her way toward his hiding place. Each time he sighted her, she was a little closer. Shortly the second rider, the one he took to be Jake Leach, reached the canyon floor and dropped from sight. The other two riders were still motionless at the narrow shelf of rock, far above. And the remaining four above could no longer be seen. Ten minutes more passed, and suddenly Christine appeared around a jagged rock formation only fifty yards away.

Raglan showed himself and waved. She swung toward him at a lope, and a moment later reined in beside him. He reached for her hand and asked, "How did it go, Chris?"

"Better than I hoped," she said. "Pa and the boys helped. Leach brought three riders with him, but the Mallorys are seeing to it that they don't follow him down here. That's Pa up on the wall, keeping one of them from following Leach. Jess and Steve took care of the other two."

"Thanks, Chris. I owe you a lot."

"Be careful. Leach will be getting suspicious by now."

"I'll handle him. You ride on."

Christine nodded, glanced anxiously back over her shoulder. Then she lifted the roan's reins. She'd just started past Raglan when Jake Leach came around the rock formation, running his horse. Catching sight of Christine, he shouted, "Hold on, you!" As she had expected, Leach had grown suspicious. That sounded in his voice, showed in his manner.

The instant after shouting, he saw Raglan. Bellowing an oath, he jerked his horse to a rearing halt. He already had his gun in his hand, and he opened fire even while his mount was rearing.

Raglan was caught off guard, confused. He didn't want to kill Leach. The man would be of no use to him dead. But it was kill or be killed, it seemed, and he swung his rifle to his shoulder. Leach's horse came down, and the man fired again. Behind Raglan, Christine cried out. He held his fire, glanced around, and saw Christine falling from the strawberry roan.

Leach's gun blasted again, and the slug struck the boulder beside Raglan and screamed as it ricocheted. The Tomahawk man was down off his horse now, diving for the cover of some rocks close to the creek bank. He fired once more as Raglan turned toward the crumpled figure of Christine.

CHAPTER EIGHTEEN

Raglan realized first that he still lived only because Leach was unnerved and his shooting consequently wild. Then he realized too that the man would soon steady himself and his aim. He was making an easy mark of himself by going to Christine, and he had to stay alive to be of any help to her—if she were not beyond help. He whirled, and at last brought his rifle into play. He drove a shot at Leach, and heard the *spang* of the slug striking the rock behind which the man crouched.

He had the hazy knowledge of four shots fired by Leach, which meant two more shots to come before the hardcase's gun was empty. He dived for the protection of the boulders beside him, and a fifth shot roared with the slug tearing at the slack of his ducking jacket. One shot more, he thought, if Leach kept his revolver fully loaded. He fired again, then deliberately exposed himself. Leach raised up, took careful aim. Raglan threw himself down as Leach squeezed the trigger. Upon the blast of the gun, he leaped up and stepped from the boulders.

"All right, Jake," he called. "That's the end of it."

Leach had failed to count his shots, and now thumbed back the six-shooter's hammer and squeezed the trigger. A panicky look spread over his tough face as he heard only a dry click of the hammer falling on a fired cartridge. He stared at the gun, then swore and threw it from him. He ran toward his horse, for the rifle on its saddle. Raglan tried to intercept him, but Leach got to the animal before him and reached across its saddle for the rifle. He had hold of its stock when Raglan swung his own rifle like a club. Leach saw it coming and ducked. He took the blow on the shoulders, saving his head, but it was powerful enough to send him reeling away from the horse without the saddle gun.

"Call it quits, damn you!"

Leach didn't heed the shout from Raglan, but whipped around in sudden flight. Raglan fired over his head, but Leach ran on. Going after him, Raglan gradually shortened his lead. They scrambled through and over rocks, plunged through brush. Leach suddenly swung around and rushed him. His heavy face was red with exertion and his breathing rasped. The man was almost spent but still dangerous. Raglan clubbed again with his rifle. The stock caught Leach full in the face, stopping him in his tracks. Leach screamed, went staggering away with his hands covering his face. Blood gushed through his fingers. He stumbled toward the creek, blindly, lost his footing and fell into the rushing water.

The current carried him between two rocks, wedging him there face down and unmoving. Raglan waded into the water, caught him by the belt, pulled him from the rocks. He dragged Leach onto the bank and left him there. He set out toward Christine at a run, but his legs began to wobble. He was far from fit, and the exertion of the past few minutes had almost done for him. He was breathless and shaky by the time he reached Christine.

He sank to his knees beside her. A little trickle of blood ran down the side of her face. He thought she was dead, she lay so still and limp. He cried out silently against that. Then he saw that there was merely a gash at her temple, not a bullet wound. He removed her scarf and went to the creek to wet it. On the way he saw the bullet crease on the rump of the strawberry roan, and understood what had happened. The roan had gone into a wild bucking because of the pain of the crease, and pitched her from the saddle. She had fallen heavily, striking her head on a rock. He returned to her and wiped her face with the wet scarf, and shortly Christine came to with a frightened little cry.

"Ed—oh, Ed!"

He lifted her to a sitting position and took her in his arms.

"Take it easy for a little while, Chris."

"I hurt. My head—"

"You had a hard bump."

"Leach, Ed? What about him?"

"I've got him," he said. "It's all right."

Christine recovered more rapidly than Leach. In a few minutes she was able to stand, and she insisted on going with Raglan when he returned to the Tomahawk man. Leach was sitting up, hunched over, holding his head in his hands. He sat in a little puddle of water, and his clothing was still dripping wet. He'd lost his hat, and his hair was stringy with dampness. He lifted his head, staring at Raglan with hate-filled eyes. His nose had stopped bleeding, but was evidently broken, for it was puffed to twice its normal size.

Raglan said, "All right, Jake. Let's do some talking."

"You go—"

"Never mind that. You're hurt, all right, but it could have been worse. I could have killed you. Maybe I should have. You've had it coming to you. But you're worth more to me alive."

Leach glared at him, saying nothing.

Raglan said, "All I want to know is one thing. Did Matt Dane give you orders to burn my buildings?"

Leach was silent, defiant.

"Jake, don't make me rough you up more," Raglan said. He waited a full minute. Then, getting no reply, he feinted a blow at the man's injured nose.

Leach flinched and jerked both hands up to protect himself. Covered up, he said, "He gave me and the others orders. Why else would we have set fire to your shacks?"

"He claims he didn't tell you to burn me out."

"How do you know he claims that?"

Raglan gestured toward Christine. "He told her."

Leach gave the girl a murky look, and said, "You Mallorys are in for it. You've asked for trouble and you'll get it."

"You're the one who's got trouble," Raglan said. "You've done your best to gun me down, but now maybe I'll do the gunning. Dane gave the orders directly to you, did he?"

"I said so, didn't I?"

"Or did he tell one of the others?"

"What the hell does it matter?"

"There were six of you. You and five others. Did Dane give you or one of the others the orders to burn me out?"

"I don't remember, Raglan," Leach said. He groaned, and again slumped forward and held his head in his hand. "What does it matter, anyway? Let me alone, Raglan!"

Raglan said, "Sure, Jake, sure."

He had learned what he needed to know. Tomahawk men had burned his buildings, apparently without orders. They'd kept it from Matthew Dane, but, as Raglan saw it, Dane, as their employer, was responsible. Now he needed to make the man admit his responsibility, and that might be difficult. He still had to get to Dane, and that meant working his way past the other Tomahawk riders. He considered the problem and arrived at the sole possible answer. Leach would have to get him through to the outfit's headquarters.

They set out a little later, Christine leading the way. Her roan was manageable despite the deep bullet crease on its rump. The sullen Leach followed her, and Raglan brought up the rear. There were no riders on the canyon wall, but, the better part of an hour later, when they came from the gorge, they saw the Mallory men standing guard over Leach's three disarmed and disgruntled companions. The Tomahawk men sat on the ground, their backs to a boulder.

Leaving his sons to stand guard, Sam Mallory came to meet Raglan and Christine and their prisoner. His lips parted in a wide grin when he saw Leach's battered face. "It worked, eh, Ed?"

"Yeah, it worked," Raglan said. "But it looks as though I've made trouble for you Mallorys."

"I reckon so. But we were willing to risk it. What's your next move?"

"I'm going to try to get through to Tomahawk headquarters."

"The hell you are! What for, man?"

"To prove to Matt Dane that his men burned my buildings. To make him see that I didn't set fire to his house for no reason at all. I'll leave it up to him, then. "He's either got to call off his wolf pack, or face a showdown between him and me."

"I don't think much of your chances, Ed."

"I do," Raglan said. "I'm taking Leach with me. If we meet any Tomahawk riders, I'll hold a cocked gun at his back. He'll take me past them."

"Risky, Ed. It's risky."

"Maybe you'll hold these three here until I've got a good start, so they can't set out to warn the others that I'm coming through."

Mallory said, "Me and the boys will hold them until nightfall. That long enough?"

Raglan said that it was, and added, "I'll warn Dane too against sending his crew to make trouble for you because of this, Sam."

"If he sends his crew, tell him there'll be shooting," Mallory said. "My boys and I will open fire on the first Tomahawk rider that comes onto our range from now on.

Raglan nodded, then said, "All right, Jake, let's go."

Leach gave him a flat, challenging stare. "This is as far as I'm going, Raglan—except alone. Make up your mind to that."

Raglan regarded him narrowly, then removed the catch-rope from his saddle-horn. He dismounted and, with Sam Mallory's help, tied Leach's hands to the pommel of his saddle. He got back onto his gray, then caught up the reins of the Tomahawk man's horse. Leach cursed him under his breath.

Mallory said, "There's one thing more, Ed. Watch out for that Association snoop, Lew Harnish. He's been prowling the Hatchets the past couple of days. Jess and Steve caught sight of him early this morning, over toward Red Larsen's ranch."

Raglan said, "I'll keep my eyes open," and started out with Leach's horse in tow. Christine rode with him.

The sun was already down, and dusk was thickening into nightfall as they emerged from the rocky hills. They rode down into the valley toward the Mallory buildings in nearly full darkness, and Raglan knew that Sam Mallory would shortly turn the three Tomahawk riders loose. He had no fear that they could overtake him. And, since the Mallorys weren't likely to return their firearms, they probably wouldn't try to trail him. Unarmed, they wouldn't want to encounter him. They would travel as fast as their mounts would go, however, to their camp outside the Hatchets to alert the rest of the Tomahawk crew so that they could try to intercept him as he came from the hills—or at least head him off before he reached the outfit's headquarters. And so there was danger for him, and his one chance of getting through lay in using Leach as a hostage.

He rode into the ranchyard with Christine, left Leach and his horse midway across it, and rode on to the corral with her.

"Just saying 'thanks' doesn't seem enough," he said. "But you know how I feel. Tell your father and brothers I'm grateful."

"I will. You'll be careful?"

"Sure. I'll get past the Tomahawk crew, and I'll settle this with Matt Dane in one way or another."

"And after that?"

"Then I'm going after Frank Amberton."

"A killing, Ed?"

"No. There won't be any gunplay between Frank and me. For one thing, he's never been any good with a gun. For another, I've got a way to force him to admit that he framed me. I can threaten to say he was the man I covered up for in that Will Vance business."

"But what good will it do just to have him admit framing you?"

"I'll work it one of two ways," he said, after a minute of thought. "I'll either take him to Matt Dane and make him say his piece with Dane as a witness, or get him to put it in writing over his signature. Don't worry, Chris. It'll work out. This is the end of it."

"I'll be waiting, Ed."

"I'll be back as soon as I can make it," he said, and turned away.

Returning to Leach, he heard a horse stamp and switch with an accompanying rattle of bit chains. He reined in at once, peering about. The sound seemed to have come from over by the house, but in the darkness he saw nothing ahead or to either side of the log building. He glanced over his shoulder at Christine. She had dismounted and he supposed her roan had made the noise.

Leach was watching him. "What's wrong, Raglan? You getting jumpy already?"

Raglan didn't answer. He kneed his gray forward and reached for the trailing reins of Leach's horse.

Leach said, "Have a heart and untie my hands, Raglan. My nose is bleeding and I've got to wipe it."

Raglan considered a moment, then decided that the man probably did feel miserable. Leach's clothes were still wet and his nose was certainly giving him trouble. He swung his gray closer to the Tomahawk man's sorrel and removed the rope. Leach pulled a bandana from his pocket and wiped away blood.

"Ride ahead of me, Jake," Raglan said. "And don't make the mistake of trying anything cute. We'll go to the next valley and then turn south through the hills. Pull up quick if we hear any riders, and keep your mouth shut. I'll have my gun on you."

Leach grunted and rode on.

Once they were clear of the yard, Raglan said, "Go on, Jake, get a move on."

They lifted their horses to a lope, but when no more than two hundred yards from the Mallory buildings Raglan heard Christine call out. Alarm rang in her voice. He said, "Pull up, Jake," and drew his gun. Leach obeyed, and Raglan swung his gray about and peered back toward the ranch buildings.

Christine called, "Behind you, Ed!"

He saw nothing at all, but heard a sudden clatter of hoofs as a rider who'd reined in when Christine called out now swung away at a lope. Then he had a glimpse of the rider, swinging wide around the house. So there had been somebody at the Mallory headquarters, he thought. And suddenly he knew who: Lew Harnish.

There was a beat of hoofs behind him, and he glanced over his shoulder to see Jake Leach in wild flight. He hesitated only a second. He wasn't riding after Leach and having an armed Harnish at his back. He kicked spurs to the gray and struck out after the range detective. He was passing the rear of the house when a gun cut loose at him, almost pointblank.

CHAPTER NINETEEN

Raglan was momentarily blinded by the muzzle flash of Harnish's gun, but the bullet didn't hit him. Then, before the detective could fire again, the gray carried him out of range. Harnish had to rein his horse about, and in the time that required Raglan regained clear vision. He wheeled his gray sharply around so Harnish couldn't bead him. Driving in against the man, Raglan struck out with his revolver. The barrel caught Harnish on the right wrist. As the gun flew from Harnish's hand, Raglan holstered his own weapon and grabbed the detective by the coat collar, hauling him from his saddle and throwing him to the ground.

Christine came running from the side of the house as Raglan dismounted. "Ed," she called. "Ed?"

"It's all right, Chris."

He stood over Harnish and said, "It looks like I've caught bigger game than I lost. Friend, you missed your chance. You should have fired when I was there in the ranchyard."

Harnish rose slowly. "Wasn't sure then it was you, Raglan."

"Well, you're sure now. And like I said, you're bigger game than Jake Leach. You're the man I've been wanting to catch. Chris, we'll take him inside and have some light. I want to see this man's face when I talk to him."

They entered by the rear door. Christine lighted the kitchen lamp. Raglan pulled a chair away from the table and told Harnish to sit down. When the man obeyed, Raglan drew his revolver and used the ejector to empty its cylinder. He let Harnish see him replace a single cartridge and spin the cylinder so that neither knew whether or not the load rested beneath the hammer. Harnish paled. He understood Raglan's intention.

Raglan took another chair and placed it about eight feet from Harnish. He straddled it, rested his arms on its back and leveled his gun at the man's middle. "Who pointed out that cow with my forged brand on it?" he said.

Harnish swallowed. "Some Tomahawk hands," he said thickly.

Raglan tilted his gun so that its muzzle beaded the man between the eyes. "Maybe I'll pull this trigger five times without anything happening," he said. "But not six times."

"I told you—"

"Chris, maybe you'd better go into another room. This won't be pretty."

"I can stand it, Ed."

"All right," Raglan said, and thumbed back the Colt's hammer. He squeezed the trigger. There was a metallic click from the gun, a cry of, "Raglan, don't!" from Harnish.

"Let's have the truth, then."

"Raglan, you won't believe the truth."

"I'll believe it, because I already know it. I know who framed me, but I want to hear it from you."

"Frank Amberton."

"You knew he was rigging a frame-up, but you went along with it?"

"No. I didn't know."

Raglan cocked his gun again.

Beads of sweat appeared on Harnish's lean face. "All right, I knew," he said. "I'll say anything you want me to say, damn you!"

"Keep talking."

"I got a message from Amberton, asking me to come to Ladder A," Harnish said. He took a handkerchief from his pocket and wiped sweat from his forehead. "I went out there and Amberton had a steer in a pen. It had a fresh RAG brand on it, and it was easy to see that it was a blotch job. It was pretty crude. It looked like a Tomahawk brand that had been worked over. Amberton didn't have any doubt about it. I took the steer to Tomahawk, and Matthew Dane had his hands kill it and take the hide off it. The Tomahawk brand showed on the inside of the hide." Harnish paused. He wiped his face again. "I figured Amberton might be framing you, but—well, it wasn't any of my business. The Association was paying my salary and Amberton was an Association member. I've always done as that crowd wanted."

Raglan glanced at Christine. "We'll put this in writing, just in case he loses his voice later on. Have you got pen and ink and paper, Chris?"

She nodded and left the room, returning shortly to put a sheet of paper, a pen and an inkwell on the table. Raglan got up, suddenly remembering that Harnish usually carried a sneak gun. He found a derringer pistol in the man's coat pocket. He gestured with his sixgun.

"Get it down on paper and sign it."

Harnish seemed calmer now. He moved his chair over to the table, picked up the pen and dipped it. He began to write in a fairly steady hand. When he had written his signature, Raglan picked up the paper and found that Harnish had written it down the way he'd told it, even to stating that he'd suspected Amberton of rigging a frame-up. When the ink was dry, Raglan folded and pocketed the paper.

"Let's go, Harnish."

"Where?"

"I'm on my way to Tomahawk," Raglan said.

He waited for the man to rise and move toward the door. Then, after a smile at Christine, he followed Harnish outside. When they reached their horses, Raglan took the rifle off Harnish's saddle and threw it aside before mounting his gray.

Raglan chose the trail. They avoided the dead Luke Chronister's valley, which would have been the shortest way from the Hatchets. They rode south for several miles through the darkness, then came down from the hills onto the undulating prairie land that formed the main portion of Tulare Basin. Raglan made Harnish rein in with him, and he listened intently for several minutes. He heard no other riders. Not knowing the exact location of the Tomahawk crew's camp, he could only guess whether or not Jake Leach had had time to reach it and turn out the other Tomahawk hands. He supposed that if Leach had alerted them, they would expect him to come from the Mallory ranch by the shortest route and so would not come this far south.

He said, "Let's go."

They struck out at a lope, and after perhaps five miles Raglan again called a halt.

"Harnish, when I show this paper of yours to Matt Dane he's going to want to know why Frank Amberton had me framed," he said. "And he'll guess at the answer—that Amberton fears me. He'll figure out why Amberton is afraid of me, and then anything can happen."

Harnish stared at him. "So what?"

"So Amberton should be warned."

"And you figure I'd want to do the warning?"

"Don't you?"

"Why should I?"

"I've a hunch that he made it worth your while to go along with his frame-up," Raglan said. "Maybe he'll make it worth your while to warn him to expect trouble.

Harnish said nothing to that.

Raglan said, "Suit yourself. It's up to you."

He kneed his gray and rode on, leaving Harnish there.

Heading toward Tomahawk, he told himself that he probably was a prize fool. A warning wasn't what Frank Amberton rated. If Matt Dane figured it out and decided to do something about Amberton, perhaps turn the Vigilantes onto him, that was no more than the Ladder A owner deserved. But Raglan remembered, if Amberton did not, the days when the two of them had been good friends ....

Just before midnight, Raglan came within sight of Tomahawk headquarters. He went in as he'd done on his last visit, fording the creek and leaving his horse in the clump of trees on the east bank. He moved less boldly this time, however; he had learned caution since that other night, and knew it was possible for Leach and some of the others to have come directly here in the hope of intercepting him. On that thought, he recalled that he had not reloaded the five empty chambers in his revolver, and halted to do so. Going on in stealthy fashion, he saw a new building, a small plank structure of one story which had been hastily erected, he supposed, as living quarters for Matthew Dane and his daughter after the burning of the ranch house.

He passed the charred wreckage of the ranch house, noticing how the two stone chimneys stood naked and lonely. He reached the rear of the plank house and saw that it had neither door nor windows at the back. He could smell the new lumber in it. He moved along the side, ducking under the one window there, which was partly open. This attempt to remain undetected went for naught, for a voice, Matt Dane's called, "Who's there?"

Raglan froze, pressing against the wall midway between the window and the front corner of the house. But at that moment a man stepped around the corner, uttering a startled grunt at sight of Raglan. Swinging toward him, Raglan thumbed back the hammer of his gun. The next instant he heard a footfall behind him, and a voice said, "We've been expecting you, bucko."

This was Jake Leach's voice.

Raglan swung toward Leach and saw two more men behind the hardcase. They ignored his gun. They kept walking in on him. He sensed the approach of the man behind him.

Leach said, "Come along, Raglan. We don't want to disturb Mr. Dane. Let's keep this nice and quiet."

Dane's lusty voice called from inside the window, "What the hell is going on out there?"

Raglan said, "Dane, it's Ed Raglan. I want a word with you."

Someone clouted him from behind. No doubt the blow was aimed for the base of his skull, but it caught him at the collar bone. His gun went off with a tremendous roar, and he reeled off balance against Jake Leach. He recovered his balance in time to dodge the clubbing blow Leach launched with his gun, and leaped away from them.

Leach snarled, "I want him alive. I want to get my hands on him!" He was panting with rage and hatred. "Raglan, the odds are against you—four to one. You haven't got a chance in hell. Throw down your gun. You hear?"

Raglan took another backward step. "My gun's on you, Jake. I'll take you with me. You're not getting your hands on me, not ever." He lifted his voice to a demanding shout. "Dane! You, Matt Dane!"

Matthew Dane appeared around the corner of the house. "All right, Raglan," he said. "I'm here. What do you want with me?"

"A talk."

"Have it."

"Not like this. Not with drawn guns."

Dane stared at him, then said, "Put them up, boys. We'll play it his way—for now. Come on inside, Raglan." His tone turned bitter. "I invite you into my home, this time—such as it is."

He spun on his heel. Raglan followed him, and Leach and the other three came after them. They all crowded into the house. Dane struck a match and lighted a lamp, revealing a small room furnished with some old, shoddy things that he must have managed to buy second-hand in Bennett. It was a sorry parlor compared to that of the destroyed ranch house. Dane remained standing by the table upon which the lamp stood. Raglan faced him, the four Tomahawk men behind him. Laurie came to the doorway across the room, a green wrapper over her nightgown and her blonde hair tousled from being abed. Her eyes were wide and frightened.

Dane said, "I'm waiting, Raglan."

"Matt, there are two matters to be discussed."

"Discuss them, then."

"Before I begin, I want you to know that I came here of my own free will," Raglan said. "Leach and these others didn't bring me. They knew I was on my way and rode here to keep me from getting to you. They've been hanging around and—"

"And we caught you sneaking around this house with a gun in your hand," Leach said. "For all I know, you were aiming to murder Mr. Dane."

Dane frowned at Leach. "What happened to your face?"

"This damn Raglan—"

"I roughed him up," Raglan cut in. "It would have been easier for me to kill him. He doesn't appreciate my letting him live, the poor fool." He took out makings and rolled and lighted a cigarette, all of them watching him. He dragged hard on his smoke. Then he said, "The first thing to be discussed is the burning of my ranch buildings. Leach and five others of your hands burned them, Matt."

Leach yelled, "That's a lie!"

The denial was loud enough, but somehow it rang as hollow as a counterfeit coin. Dane looked long at Leach, his ruddy face stiff with anger.

Raglan said, "Matt, if I'd burned your house first, you sure as shooting would have burned mine in retaliation. You would have claimed there was justification. I'm claiming that now. And I'm asking you to end this feud between the two of us. I'm asking you to call off Leach and the rest of your crew."

There was a taut silence.

Laurie broke it. "He's got the right to ask that, Dad. And you—you should do as he asks."

Dane said, "Raglan, you're still a rustler."

"That's the second matter to be discussed," Raglan said. He took Harnish's deposition from his pocket and held it out to Dane. "This will clear up that rustling charge against me. I was framed, Matt, and you were hoodwinked."

Dane accepted the paper with some reluctance, unfolded it, held it close to the lamp, and scowled over its brief message. When he looked up, he gestured at Leach and the others.

"Get out," he said. "This is the end of it. If any Tomahawk hand molests Raglan from now on, he'll answer to me. One of you ride out and tell the rest of the crew to come in. The other three go to the bunkhouse and turn in.

They went out, Jake Leach seeming anxious to get away. The last man out closed the door. And Ed Raglan heaved a sigh of relief, telling himself that it was over at last. Then he saw the ugly gleam in Matthew Dane's eyes, and knew this wasn't the end of it.

CHAPTER TWENTY

It was clear to Raglan that Dane wanted no witnesses to this scene. He said, "Laurie, how about making some coffee for us?" He waited until his daughter went to the kitchen, and then he asked sharply,

"How did you get Harnish to sign this thing?"

Raglan shrugged. "The how of it doesn't matter, Matt."

"If you used threats or violence, it's not worth a damn. He'll repudiate it."

"I'm not worried about that."

"Harnish says he suspected Amberton of rigging a frame-up. Suspected."

"Quit hedging, Matt. This clears me and you've got to admit it."

Dane went and sat on a spindly straight-backed chair. It creaked under his bulk. He'd pulled on shirt and pants before making his appearance, but his shirt was unbuttoned and he wore carpet slippers on his feet. He was not at his best advantage now, and Raglan saw little that was formidable about him.

Dane said, "Frank Amberton and you used to be good friends."

"That's right."

"A man wouldn't frame his friend."

"A man would be apt to cover up for his friend, if he found evidence that his friend was a rustler," Raglan said. "One way or another, it looks as though Frank no longer thinks much of our friendship."

"Why'd he frame you, Raglan?"

"You're admitting there was a frame-up?"

Dane gave him a scowl. "Raglan, I never liked you from the day you and I had trouble over my daughter. You know that. It was a long time ago and maybe Laurie was more to blame than you. But I still don't like you. You're too damn proud and arrogant for a man who owns no more than he can carry on a horse. Still, I'm giving you the benefit of the doubt. I'll admit it looks like you were framed. Now why did Frank Amberton frame you?"

"Matt, my one-time friendship means something to me, even if it doesn't to Frank," Raglan said. "All I want is to clear my name of that rustler charge."

"It's not enough."

"It is for me."

Dane shook his head. "You're seeing it through," he said. "There's only one reason why Amberton would be out to get you. He was scared of you."

Raglan puffed on his cigarette, saying nothing.

Dane went on, "The night of the party here at Tomahawk, you said you'd let that rustler, Will Vance, go because the man you were covering up for was a big-outfit man. The only big-outfit man you'd cover up for is Frank Amberton—which is something I should have figured out long ago. So you covered up for him, but he wasn't sure you'd keep on covering up. He got worried, scared, and to discredit you—to break you—he rigged that frame-up."

Still Raglan did not speak.

"That's something more I should have figured out," Dane said. "Amberton came along too fast, grew too big in too big a hurry. Yes, I should have known—from the way he lives, by the amount of money he spends. He lives as well as I do, and I've been in the cattle business for thirty years. Raglan, I hate a cow thief like I hate the Devil himself."

"You don't have to tell me that," Raglan said. "I know. I know what happened to poor Bart Somers—and to some others. I know how you had your gunhands hunt for me. But I'll tell you this, Matt. There are worse things than cow thieves."

"If you're trying to tell me to overlook Amberton's being one—"

I'm the man who should bear the grudge against him. He framed me. He cost me my job at Seventy-seven Ranch, and my reputation as an honest man. Before that, he sent a bushwhacker to try to kill me." Raglan went to the door, opened it and threw his cigarette butt outside. Facing Dane again, he went on, "Maybe I should take a gun and go after him. Somehow, I can't. If I can overlook his trying to have me murdered and his framing me, you should be able to overlook his rustling."

"And let him go on with his stealing?"

"He'll quit it now, with it known."

"Once a man turns bad, he stays bad."

"I don't agree, Matt. And like I said, there are worse things than cow thieves."

Dane squinted at him. "You keep saying that. What are you getting at?"

Raglan rested his arms on the back of a chair, leaned forward and leveled his index finger at the older man. "Matt, this is a showdown all the way through. I'm going to have it out with you, and you're not going to like it. But I'm your match, and maybe more than your match. I—"

"Quit your bragging and get it said."

"All right. I say that any man who masks his face and calls himself a Vigilante and takes the law into his own hands is worse than any rustler or law-breaker."

"When there's no law on a range—"

"There's never been a Vigilante movement that didn't give somebody a chance to grind his own axe," Raglan cut in. "And that's what you've been doing. The main part of the Basin has got too crowded to suit you. You can't drive out the big outfits, so you decided to drive out the two-bit ranchers and take over their Hatchet Hills range. You used the Vigilantes for just that. I don't know if you were the man who turned them loose on Luke Chronister, but I'm pretty sure you turned them loose on old J. C. Pierce—a man too frail with age to do any rustling." He lifted his voice when Dane opened his mouth to argue. "You tried to buy Pierce's Red Butte range. When he wouldn't sell, you put his name on the Vigilante list and now he's in his grave."

He expected a violent outburst, but Dane merely sat there with his hands on his knees. The man had lost some of his florid coloring. He'd dropped Harnish's deposition. Raglan picked it up and pocketed it.

Dane said, "That's how it looks to you, eh?"

"How else could it look?"

"If I'm on trial, I should have a chance to defend myself."

"I'm listening."

Dane was silent a moment, apparently trying to collect his thoughts. "I guess I always knew, in the back of my mind, that it was a dangerous business. But something had to be done about the rustling. It was getting to be on too large a scale. But I was after thieves like Bart Somers—the professionals. I tell you this, Raglan. I swear it. I never had any idea of making war on the Hatchet Hills ranchers."

"Luke Chronister is in his grave. So is J. C. Pierce."

"I had nothing to do with what happened to them."

"Jake Leach was along the night old Pierce was killed."

Dane's astonishment seemed genuine. "You're sure of that?"

Raglan nodded. "He showed his face when he shouted a threat at me."

All the bluster had gone out of Matthew Dane. He shook his head remorsefully. "Then some of the blame is mine, just as I've got to shoulder some of the blame for my men burning your buildings. I was hoodwinked by Amberton, like you said, and I've been hoodwinked by Leach and maybe some others of my crew. I didn't know they were doing all that night riding. It looks as though I'll have to do some weeding out, starting with Leach."

"Matt, it would be better if you found out the why of it."

"The reason Leach and the others—if there were others from my crew—rode with the Vigilantes? I can tell you the reason. I took some of them along when I led the Vigilantes on a couple of raids—against real rustlers, mind you—and they liked it. They've done it since, if you really saw Leach at Pierce's place, just for the sport of it."

"Some sport, Matt. Who led the Vigilantes that night?"

"I don't know. I wasn't told about their going to Pierce's, before or after. I heard about the fight there second-handed, from my crew."

"Hank Mockridge got killed that night."

"So I heard. And I can tell you about Hank."

"What about him?"

"He was another one who liked the Vigilantes, for the hell of it—for the sport. He liked those hangings, Raglan."

Raglan sighed heavily. "Well, he had his fun and paid for it. But why did he and the others go after old Pierce? Just for the sport of it?"

"I don't know," Dane said. "I organized the Vigilantes. That much I'll admit. But somehow somebody else took the reins out of my hands, almost without my knowing it. Maybe I'm getting old and easy to fool."

Laurie came into the room with a tray. She served Raglan first, saying, "Ed, I guess you know that Christine Mallory was here to see Dad and me." She smiled. "She's really something, for a back-country girl."

"Yes," he said. "Really something."

"And in love with you, too."

"I'm a lucky dog."

"I suppose you are," she said. She looked wistful, proving that in some ways Laurie was not wholly grown up. "But she's not doing so badly. She's getting just about the best man on this range. I should have such luck. Take something to eat along with your coffee, Ed." She laughed. "If the way to a man's heart is through his stomach, maybe this will make me Christine's rival."

He took a sandwich along with a cup of coffee, then watched Laurie go to serve her father. He didn't know whether she was in earnest or not. He hoped she wasn't, for so far as he was concerned not she nor any other woman would be Christine's rival.

He sat down at last, and the food reminded him that he hadn't eaten since breakfast. The sandwich consisted of cold roast beef between thick slices of bread. The coffee was hot and strong. He relaxed in the chair, stretched his long legs. He felt content. Here he was, a guest in the home of the biggest cattleman in Tulare Basin—one of the biggest anywhere. He had been accepted as an equal by Matthew Dane, and that was his due. He'd outfought and outsmarted Tomahawk, and he'd made its owner say "uncle." With Dane's help, he would clear his name so far as the other big-outfit men were concerned. He had his Squaw Creek range, and his cattle, and the mavericks waiting for his RAG brand. He would grow, grow as big as Matthew Dane. He would rebuild his headquarters, make it a fine one this time. Best of all, Christine was waiting for him. He could see her now, in the new house he would build, as his wife. She was the proper sort of mate for a man as lusty as himself. Together, they would build his Squaw Creek Ranch into a worthwhile outfit. Maybe one day Christine would give him a fine son or two, and perhaps a beautiful daughter.

He roused from his reverie to see Laurie sitting across the room sipping coffee and eyeing him in that wistful fashion. He saw that Dane had eaten nothing, and was brooding over his still nearly full cup of coffee.

Dane said, "You've talked a lot, Raglan. You've had your say. You've made me see some of my blunders. So what's the answer?"

"Break up the Vigilantes," Raglan said. "Get rid of that Association detective, Lew Harnish. Make some sort of a deal at the county seat, with the sheriff's office, so that there's an efficient, honest deputy sent out to the Basin. Let the Association pay the deputy's salary, if he comes high. Or pay it yourself."

Dane nodded. "I'll give it some thought. But what about Frank Amberton?"

Raglan flinched, mentally. He had known that the Tomahawk owner would bring the talk around to Amberton again. He set to thinking about it. He didn't know the answer, where his one-time friend was concerned. Amberton had tried to have him murdered, had had him branded thief. Still, he didn't want to see him hanged for his rustling. And he knew the stubborn streak of Matthew Dane. Before breaking up the Vigilantes, Dane might lead them to Ladder A one night. And if Harnish hadn't warned Amberton or if the warning was ignored … Raglan heard a sudden hard drumming of hoofs as a rider left Tomahawk ranch-yard. The sound roused Dane from his chair and took him to the door.

"Who rode out?" Dane called to one of his men over at the bunkhouse.

Raglan heard the reply: "Jake Leach."

"Where's he going?"

Raglan didn't catch the answer to the second question, but when Matthew Dane turned from the door his face was ugly with rage.

"That does it, Raglan," he said. "Leach gathered his gear together and cleared out."

"Well, you said you were going to weed him out This saves you the bother."

"He told Pete Archer he's going to Ladder A."

"Ladder A? Why?"

"That's what I intend to find out," Dane said. "He and Frank Amberton are in cahoots. Why Amberton made a deal with a rider on my payroll is something I'm going to find out—tonight."

He strode off to his bedroom.

Laurie rose, came to Raglan and took the cup from his hand. "Ed, I'm scared. If he goes to Ladder A and makes accusations against Frank Amberton and Jake Leach, anything can happen. Go with him, won't you?"

"I intend to, Laurie," Raglan said wearily.

He picked up his hat and left the house to get his horse. This had been inevitable from the start, he thought bitterly. Try as he might, he hadn't been able to buck a line of fate that was written on the books. He was heading for a delayed showdown with Frank Amberton. Nothing could stop it now.

CHAPTER TWENTY ONE

They rode through the darkness at a steady lope, Matthew Dane resolute to the point of grimness. Raglan thought it odd that Dane should be so determined on a showdown with Frank Amberton, since all Dane had against Ladder A's owner was a knowledge of his thievery and his having some sort of understanding with Jake Leach. That seemed so little in comparison to what Raglan had against Amberton, yet he, Raglan, was the reluctant rider.

Raglan even clung to the hope that Harnish had warned Amberton; that Amberton, heeding the warning, had done the sensible thing and cleared out. But finally they topped a rise of ground and saw the lighted windows at Ladder A, and he knew that they would find Amberton at home.

They rode into the ranchyard about ten minutes after seeing the lights. The big, fine house alone was lighted. The bunkhouse was dark. A cowpony stood before the house, a bedroll and a warsack tied behind its saddle. The horse Jake Leach had ridden, Raglan supposed. They dismounted and left their horses ground hitched. Raglan followed Dane onto the porch and stood aside as the old man rapped heavily upon the door with his knuckles.

Clara came to the door, clad as she'd been on Raglan's last visit here in wrapper, nightgown and slippers. Dane said, "Mrs. Amberton, I want to see your husband. I take it that he's up, even though it is an ungodly hour."

He pushed past Clara as he spoke.

There was no light in the hall, so Raglan, entering after Dane, couldn't make out the woman's expression. But he sensed her fear. She closed the door and caught Raglan by the arm before he could follow Dane into the parlor.

"Ed, please—"

"I'll do what I can, Clara."

"Everything's going wrong. I'm frightened."

"Keep Frank from playing the fool," he said. "I'll try to handle Dane,"

He turned from her, entered the enormous, luxuriously furnished parlor.

Dane had halted in the center of the room, facing Amberton and Leach who were standing before the fireplace at the far end of the room. Amberton was fully dressed, except for his hat, and from that Raglan knew that Harnish had indeed visited Ladder A. Amberton had been about to clear out and Leach's arrival, no doubt only minutes ago, had delayed him. At sight of Raglan, Amberton's eyes clouded. Clara came into the room, and stood beside her husband.

Dane said, "Frank, I wanted to catch you and Jake together. I didn't want to give you a chance to send him on his way and lie about being hand-in-glove with him when I questioned you later. What's between you two?"

It was Clara who answered. "There's nothing between them. Jake came here and asked Frank to give him a job. He said he'd fallen out with you."

"At three in the morning?" Dane gave a snort. "You'll have to do better than that, Mrs. Amberton. Maybe you'd better let your husband do the talking."

"It's nothing, Matt," Amberton said. "Nothing at all."

"You make a deal with one of my riders, and have the gall to say it's nothing?" Dane swore. "The game's over, Frank. You should have known it wasn't one that would last, or that you could win." He shifted his angry gaze to Leach. "You, Jake. What's between you and Amberton?"

Leach's face with its enormously swollen nose resembled a clown's mask, but, standing there with his thumbs hooked in his gunbelt, he looked dangerous rather than clownish. "It's like Mrs. Amberton said. I came here for a job. Take it or leave it, old man."

"I'm not taking it or leaving it," Dane said. "Amberton's a cow thief, but he's too biggety to do the actual stealing. You and some others did it for him. You collected your wages from Tomahawk, but you kept busy branding cattle for Ladder A. Hell, Jake, I can see what's right before my nose."

"All right," Leach said. "What are you figuring on doing about it?"

Raglan regarded the man with surprise, wondering about this voluntary admission of guilt. Jake Leach seemed a bit too sure of himself. Raglan suddenly went wary. Amberton was less sure of himself, however. Leach's admission hit him hard. He sank into a chair, lowering his head into his hands. Clara frowned, and it seemed to Raglan that she was annoyed by this show of weakness in her husband. She looked at Dane defiantly.

"It's not like it seems," she said. "Frank didn't start out to do wrong. But he got into debt, so deep in debt that there was no other way out. He gambled and lost, and now he's quitting the game."

"What makes him think he can quit," Dane said, "without paying the piper?"

"He'll be paying enough, if he leaves Ladder A."

"So he's going to leave, is he?"

Raglan said, "Matt, that's how it's going to be."

Clara gave him a grateful glance, but Dane scowled.

"You sure like to turn the other cheek when you're slapped," Dane said. "You've made up your mind that he's to be let off scot free, have you?"

Raglan shrugged. "Like Mrs. Amberton says, he'll be paying plenty by leaving Ladder A." He looked at Amberton. "Frank, I'll back you up on that. It's more than you rate from me, but since we used to be friends I'll do it. But first you're going to make a clean breast of it. You understand?"

Amberton lifted his head slowly. "What do you want me to say?" he said. "You know it all. At least, all you want to know. But I'm not as guilty as you think. Leach is as much to blame as I am. And Lew Harnish more."

"That's right," Dane said. "Shift the blame onto somebody else."

Raglan said, "What about Leach and Harnish, Frank?"

"At the start," Frank Amberton said huskily, "I hired Will Vance and three other men down on their luck to maverick for me. But the mavericks were getting scarce. So I got them to do some brand changing for me. Leach caught on first. He came on one of my men changing the Tomahawk brand on a cow into a Ladder A."

Matthew Dane cursed him.

Amberton went on, "Leach stopped me in town one day and told me how he'd caught one of my men. He said he'd do some brand changing for me, at ten dollars a head. I don't know if he ever put any cattle into my Ladder A brand, but he made me pay him fifty dollars a week. Sure, I was paying him to keep quiet. He blackmailed me. But he was a piker compared to Lew Harnish."

"How much did Harnish want to keep quiet, Frank?" Raglan asked.

"He just about took over," Amberton said bitterly. "He told me I'd better take him on as my silent partner. Silent, hell. It got so that he was running things, doing the planning, giving me orders." He shot Dane an angry look. "You brought him here to work for the Association. A man like that."

"So I'm to blame, am I?" Dane said. "Not by a long shot."

Raglan felt a sudden draft on the back of his neck, but he was so intent upon Amberton that he did not wonder about the reason for it.

He said, "Get on with it, Frank."

Amberton shook his head hopelessly. "You won't believe this, Ed. But I'll tell it. After you told me about catching Will Vance, that night of the party at Tomahawk, I decided to call it quits. I figured I might be able to pay off my debts in a few years if I was careful of my money. I told Harnish that same night, but he wouldn't have it that way. He saw himself getting rich and he wasn't giving up a good thing. He said that if you were the only one who knew about my—my rustling, he'd take care of you."

"So it was Harnish who tried to bushwhack me in the Hatchets?"

"Yes. I didn't know about it until afterwards, when he told me."

Raglan didn't know whether to believe that or not, but he said, "Go on."

"Harnish said we'd have to get you in another way, because you were too tough and smart to be bushwhacked. He rigged the frame-up."

"But you went along with it, Frank."

"I had to. He threatened to expose me as a rustler." Amberton paused, looking as though he wanted to be believed and feared he was thought a liar. "He figured the frame-up would get you killed or scare you out of Tulare Basin. When Tomahawk wasn't able to hunt you down or drive you out, Harnish got the Vigilantes to do something about you. When they got nowhere, he set out to look for you. You know what came of that. You got the best of him."

"You been riding with the Vigilantes, Frank?"

"Not lately. Only when Matt did."

"What made you drop out?"

Amberton shrugged. "I wasn't asked along, and wouldn't have gone if I'd been asked. Hank Mockridge and some others started jumping men they couldn't prove were rustlers, just out of orneriness."

"Men like Luke Chronister and J. C. Pierce?"

Amberton nodded.

Raglan looked at Matthew Dane. "That does it, Matt," he said. "We've got the whole rotten mess explained. Like I said, the Vigilantes turned out to be worse than the rustlers. And your man, Harnish, is the worst of the lot."

Dane frowned. "Now you're asking me to forgive and forget that Frank was a thief," he said. "You've swallowed his story, hook, line and sinker. Me, I'm not so sure but that he's as slick a liar as he is a rustler."

Behind them, from the hall doorway, a new voice said, "So what do you figure on doing with him, Mr. Dane?"

Even before he swung around, Raglan knew he would see Lew Harnish with a cocked gun in his hand.

He completed his turn, and that's how it was.

Harnish lounged there in the doorway, his gun leveled and an unlighted cheroot in his mouth. Raglan took several backward steps to the side of the room. He did this without conscious thought, and stopped only when Harnish said, "That's far enough, Raglan."

Raglan halted, but saw that Matthew Dane, after turning, had done as he had done and now stood at the opposite side of the room. They were covered by Harnish's weapon, true. But if one or the other drew his fire by grabbing for a gun, the other might be able to down Harnish. The same thought must have occurred to Dane, for he looked at Raglan and nodded. It was certain death for one of them, however, and Raglan shook his head.

"Let him have his say, Matt," he said. "He's primed to crow a little."

"Sure," Harnish said. "Let's all be reasonable."

"What's your deal, Lew?" Raglan remembered that draft he'd felt some minutes ago, and cursed his stupidity in not guessing that it had been created by the opening of the outside door. He should have known that someone had entered the house. Yes, he should have suspected that Harnish might be around. "Is that it?" he said. "You've got a deal that'll satisfy all of us?"

"Maybe," Harnish said. "You might as well hear it."

Raglan watched him take a match from his coat pocket, with his left hand while his right kept the revolver leveled. He lighted the match with his thumbnail, then held the flame to his cheroot. His eyes and his gun never wavered from Raglan. A clammy sweat broke out on Raglan. He feared that Dane would start something while he was beaded like that.

His cheroot burning, Harnish said, "I was just about to ride out when I heard you and Dane riding in. I pulled my horse around behind the barn and wondered what you were up to. When no shooting happened, I figured our friend, Frank here, was doing a lot of talking."

Raglan had the feeling that Harnish was stalling, bidding for time. He wondered why, and then he understood. Harnish realized that he could shoot down only Raglan or Dane, and that the survivor would get him. He was trying to find a way out. That Harnish wanted them both killed was a certainty, of course. By getting rid of them, the man evidently figured, he and Frank Amberton could continue their stealing on an even larger scale.

Harnish said, "Frank, get smart. With these two taken care of, neither of us will have to run. We'll be set up here for life."

Raglan glanced across the room. Amberton rose, a sickly pallor on his face. He reached out his arm and pushed Clara away from him, as though wanting her out of danger. Jake Leach stood there stonily, to one side of Amberton, his hand on the butt of his holstered gun.

After a moment Amberton said, "I've got no gun, Lew. I gave you mine."

"Get another."

"I've got none here in the house."

Raglan looked back at Harnish. "You'll get no help there, Lew. Frank never was much of a hand with a gun. You know, you're a dead man, Lew. The second you pull that trigger, you're a dead man." He paused, watching the man intently. He saw a slight frown come to Harnish's face. "You're not such a hand with a gun, yourself, Harnish. Remember how you missed me that day in the Hatchet Hills and tonight over at the Mallory place?"

"The range is short now, Raglan," Harnish said. "Jake, take a hand. It'll be worth your while."

Leach said, "Maybe worth my while—if we get away with it."

"We'll get away with it," Harnish told him. "Our story will be that Dane accused Raglan of being a rustler. Then Raglan killed him—and we killed Raglan trying to keep him from killing Dane." He took the cheroot from his mouth, and threw it to the floor. "You've been after Raglan for a long time. Now's your chance, Jake. Take it, man!"

Raglan glanced around the room. Dane gave him a jerky nod, his face grim. Jake Leach had his gun half drawn. Frank Amberton was staring at Leach, moving toward him.

Raglan looked back at Harnish, saw him swinging his gun toward Dane.

He drew, and he fired the instant his gun cleared its holster.

Harnish's gun racketed, and Leach's.

The room seemed to rock with the shots. Dane wasn't hit, but Harnish was. Swaying, slowly collapsing, Harnish turned his gun back toward Raglan. Before he could steady it, Dane's gun crashed. Harnish's second shot went into the floor, then he went down. Raglan whirled toward Leach, saw him and Amberton struggling against each other. Leach suddenly broke free of Amberton, but stumbled over a hassock and fell to the floor. In a fit of rage, he drove a wild shot at Amberton. Missing it, he started to fire again. Raglan drove a shot at him. Leach was rising as the slug hit him, and it bowled him over onto his side. He made a desperate attempt to pick himself up, then lost his gun. The next moment he sprawled out and, like Harnish, did not move again.

The room was hazy with powder smoke, and jarringly quiet.

Raglan glanced at Matthew Dane. The old man seemed all right. Clara went to Amberton, threw herself into his arms, and clung to him making whimpering sounds.

Raglan felt himself shaking. His gun rattled against leather as he holstered it.

Half a dozen Ladder A cowhands burst into the house, none fully dressed but all armed. Amberton explained that the trouble was over, and got them to remove the two dead men. By the time they were gone, Matthew Dane had made his decision.

He said, "You've earned another chance, Frank. Take it. But if you step out of line again, I'll make you wish you'd never seen this range." He looked at Raglan. "Coming, Ed?"

Raglan grunted assent, but lingered after Dane left the room. He smiled wryly at Frank and Clara Amberton. "You've learned your lesson, both of you. Don't forget it."

Still badly shaken, Amberton merely nodded.

Clara said, "There's no danger of that, Ed," and Raglan left them.

He and Matt Dane rode at a lope for several miles, then slowed to a walk. There was a trace of dawn in the sky behind them. Raglan rolled and lighted a cigarette, drew the smoke deep into his lungs. Exhaled, it sounded like a sigh. They had not spoken since leaving Ladder A, but Raglan felt friendly toward Matthew Dane and knew that the feeling was mutual. That was odd, he reflected, after they had been enemies for so many years.

Finally, when they came within sight of Tomahawk headquarters, Dane said, "Ed, we were lucky. The more I think about it, the more I can't see how at least one of us didn't get killed."

"Well, Frank's switching over gave us just the edge we needed."

"Yeah. And I didn't expect him to switch, any more than Harnish did. I'll have to admit I was wrong in saying that once a man turns bad he stays bad."

Raglan smiled thinly. "I guess you will, Matt," he said.

But he wasn't so sure that it had been a change of heart on Frank Amberton's part. He suspected that Amberton had jumped Jake Leach not so much because he wanted to play it square, but because he'd been smart enough to see that if Leach and Harnish won out, he would be saddled with them forever. True, Amberton was likely to stay honest from now on. But only because of fear. Without a doubt, he would remember the easy money, and in the future he'd have to fight temptation. Frank Amberton was weak. Raglan hoped that he was so weak that his fear would always be greater than his greed, because it wasn't likely that there would be a way out for him a second time.

It was gray dawn when they reached Tomahawk headquarters. Dane invited Raglan to stop and have breakfast and get some rest, but he, though both hungry and tired, was anxious to return to the Hatchet Hills. Christine would be wondering, worrying. He wanted to reassure her. He needed to see her. So he turned down the invitation and asked for a fresh mount.

He roped a dun gelding in the Tomahawk corral, shifted the saddle from his gray to it. He turned the gray into the corral, telling Dane that he would come back for it one day soon. He mounted the dun at once, but then held it in and looked down at Matthew Dane.

"Matt, I'm sorry about burning your house," he said. "I guess you know that."

"I can build another. Like you said, you were justified. Forget it."

"No hard feelings, then?"

"No. But there's one thing, Ed. I've got a job here for you, a foreman's job."

Raglan chuckled. "I've learned one thing from this mess, Matt," he said. "I'm capable of being my own man. But thanks anyway."

"It's a hard row to hoe, being a raggedy-pants cowman."

"That's something I'm not going to be for long."

Dane studied him for a spell. Then he said, "That I can believe. Good luck."

Raglan said, "Thanks again, Matt," and turned the dun away.

He rode west at a lope, the new day unfolding bright and wonderful across the land and all about him. At midmorning he rode into the valley where the Mallory ranch was located, and as he approached the buildings he saw Sam Mallory and his sons come to the edge of the ranchyard to welcome him. He knew that they too had been wondering and worrying about him, and the knowledge that he was not without friends added to his sense of well-being.

He reined in and dismounted. "It's over and done with," he said. "There'll be no more trouble."

"Good," Sam Mallory said. "Chris is waiting to hear that."

He took the dun's reins from Raglan's hand.

She did not appear at the door to welcome him. She sat waiting in the parlor, wearing her best dress and a ladylike demeanor. She looked like a young woman expecting a caller, a favored suitor, and hoping that the courting would end now with a proposal. He halted just inside the door, removing his hat and smiling. It was an odd hour for romance. Besides, a man tired to the core and needing a shave and a scrubbing with yellow soap was hardly eligible to do any courting.

But Christine was beautiful in his eyes, and he marveled that she was his for the mere asking. He needed to do no asking, however, because Christine forgot to be a proper lady welcoming a gentleman caller. She cried, "Ed! Oh, Ed!" and ran straight into his arms.
